MAKING LOVE

Lucretia Stewart

MAKING LOVE

a romance

The University of Wisconsin Press
Terrace Books

Róm
Stewart

The University of Wisconsin Press
1930 Monroe Street
Madison, Wisconsin 53711

www.wisc.edu/wisconsinpress/

5   4   3   2   1

Printed in the United States of America

Library of Congress Cataloging-in-Publication Data
Stewart, Lucretia, 1952–
Making love : a romance / Lucretia Stewart.
p. cm.
ISBN 0-299-19920-7 (pbk.: alk. paper)
1. Single women—Fiction. 2. Fathers—Death—Fiction. 3. London
(England)—Fiction. I. Title.
PR6069.T4597M35   2004
823'.914—dc22   200362154

Terrace Books, a division of the University of Wisconsin Press,
takes its name from the Memorial Union Terrace, located at the
University of Wisconsin–Madison. Since its inception in 1907,
the Wisconsin Union has provided a venue for students, faculty,
staff, and alumni to debate art, music, politics, and the issues of
the day. It is a place where theater, music, drama, dance, outdoor
activities, and major speakers are made available to the campus
and the community. To learn more about the Union, visit
www.union.wisc.edu.

For Edmund White, with love

Acknowledgements

I acknowledge and am grateful for the support of the Authors' Foundation. I am also grateful to the following: Rebecca Carter, Deborah Rogers, Holly Eley, David Miller, Jonathan Burnham and Michael Carroll.

In addition, I would like to thank Hugo Williams for permission to use the lines from his poem 'Broken Dreams'. I also acknowledge the use of lines from D. J. Enright's poem 'Making Love', courtesy of Chatto and Windus and Watson, Little Ltd.; Josephine Balmer's translation of Sappho from *Sappho: Poems and Fragments* (Bloodaxe) and Archibald Colquhoun's translation of Lampedusa's *The Leopard* (Harvill Press). The lines from Rudyard Kipling's 'The Virginity' are quoted with the kind permission of A. P. Watt Ltd. on behalf of the National Trust for Places of Historic Interest or Natural Beauty. Thanks also to Farrar, Straus & Giroux for permission to quote lines from Derek Walcott's 'Endings', *Collected Poems*.

Making love —
Love was what they'd made.
In rooms here and there,
In this town and that.

from 'Making Love' by D. J. Enright

Part One

Try as he will, no man breaks wholly loose
From his first love, no matter who she be . . .
We've only one virginity to lose,
And where we lost it there our hearts will be!

from 'The Virginity' by Rudyard Kipling

One

In London, two days after my father's funeral, I began an affair with a man with whom I had first slept twenty-five years earlier in Italy. He claimed then, and subsequently continued to claim, that I was the first woman he had ever slept with.

I've never been quite sure why I didn't entirely believe him. Perhaps because what he said is what you would say if you wanted to get someone into bed. On the other hand, what else could account for the fact that Louis, on some fundamental level, had remained, if not continuously, then certainly recurrently, over a period of twenty-five years (and despite girlfriends and a marriage which survived for ten years), obsessed with me.

When I asked Louis why he had called me, why *now*, he said: 'I wanted to see if I was still in love with you.'

'And are you?'

'Yes, I think I am.'

How could I possibly resist?

We first met one Christmas in Athens, where our fathers were both stationed. Louis' father had only recently arrived, while my own father had been in Greece for several years and was, as it happened, about to leave. They overlapped for a few wintery months.

My father was Louis' father's boss; the boss, in fact, of the whole show, which gave him (gave us) a privileged way of life. We lived in a big, white house, the entrance of which was flanked with fluted columns, like those of the Parthenon. Recently, going through a box of my father's old papers, I found a brown envelope full of photographs of this house. Its sheer grandeur, which I had forgotten, gave me a shock. The hall, with its four sets of double doors edged in gold, would not have looked out of place at Versailles or at Blenheim. The polished marble stairway had a perfect crimson stair carpet and pairs of purple brocade thrones stood at regular, formal intervals against the ivory-coloured walls. Four crystal chandeliers were suspended from the high ceiling whose mouldings were picked out in gold, as was the elaborate cornice. At one end of the room hung a huge full-length portrait by Augustus John of Madame Suggia, the cellist, in a red silk evening dress. This picture, which depicted her bent over her cello, dominated the long hall, which was so big that it could have served as a ballroom – and indeed sometimes did.

I don't remember how many rooms the house contained. Lots, I know – I had a suite of rooms in the basement consisting of a bedroom, a little sitting-room and a bathroom. I do recall, though, that if I ever dropped an item of clothing, even a handkerchief, it would immediately be picked up and whisked away, then returned to me within hours, washed and immaculately ironed by one of the servants.

The servants ... How many of them were there? I remember a chauffeur; a butler; two footmen; a full-time seamstress; at least four housemaids and an ancient chef who had once worked as a kitchen boy for the last Czar of Russia. The old man made a wonderful meringue pudding, which he decorated with spun sugar as fine as Venetian glass. I always asked for it on the first and last days of the school holidays.

I met Louis during the holidays, over what was to be my last Christmas in Athens. I was just eighteen, Louis barely seventeen. Whatever he may have felt about me at the time, I certainly didn't think of him as a potential lover. I saw him more as a companion, someone to hang out with, a kind of more interesting younger brother. He would visit me in the afternoons; we'd drink tea, play records and talk about poetry — flirtation disguised as bookishness. Sometimes he would try to kiss me but I always pushed him away. If I fancied anyone in Athens, it was Louis' older brother.

It was the thing among my set at school to describe boys (and we almost never talked about anything else) as 'pretty' — as if they were parrots, or dresses. Louis' brother was definitely pretty, flirtatious too. He once told me at a party that my eyes had a post-orgasmic expression. Not true, I'm afraid. Anyhow, I knew his flirting didn't mean anything; he had a girlfriend back in London. I suppose Louis was also pretty. He was tall and slender with thick, springy, brown hair and fine, regular features.

Late one afternoon, I came home with him after a walk and found my parents sitting with a couple of their friends in the small drawing-room, the informal, family one where Thomas Phillips's famous portrait of Byron in Albanian costume hung. In early January, the air was cold and our cheeks were pink. We had walked all the way down to Monasteraki, the old market district below the Acropolis, and back again. Louis' face was flushed, not just with the fresh air, but also with excitement, possibly with the excitement of being with me and from the pleasure of our expedition. He loved Greece, he loved old things and, perhaps, he loved me. When Louis left the room, my father's friend, an English writer who lived in Greece, said: 'Isn't he beautiful? Like the young Alexander the Great.'

But I couldn't see it. I wasn't interested. To me, he was a younger boy, and we were only interested in boys who were nineteen, or twenty, or older. And we wanted them to be sophisticated. Louis wasn't. He was just young, and very clever, and sweet.

I had lost my virginity almost exactly a year before, three weeks after my seventeenth birthday, to a boy I had met at a Hallowe'en party. It was one of those uneasy parties made up of sulky teenagers and irritated parents, an ill-advised generational mix in which each side resented the other. The boy, whose name was Damon, had green eyes with thick, fringed lashes and thick, reddish-brown hair. He was eighteen and had just left Eton.

All through the second half of the winter term, I would take the train up to London whenever I could get away on Sundays, in order to see him at the flat which he shared in Earl's Court with another ex-Etonian. They were both students at a crammer, retaking their A levels and trying to get into some university or other. Sometimes Fleur, my best friend, would come too and we would all lie around on the floor on grimy cushions and smoke dope. Once Damon came down to see me at school and I walked about a mile to meet him at the little station. There was nothing for us to do there except trudge around the cold countryside. There wasn't even a tea-shop.

In London Damon would always try to get me into bed but I was wary. Virginity didn't seem like a burden to me. If it had, I could have shed it easily enough. One of the perks of my father's job was a house by the sea. There, I had spent the previous summer doing everything imaginable – except that – with the younger son of our Greek neighbours. Around midnight my father would come out on to the terrace and call me, as if I were a dog or a cat, and I would crawl out of the bushes and come home, dishevelled and flushed after hours of heavy petting. But Vassili was a well-brought-up Greek boy; he neither insisted nor begged for more. Probably he couldn't believe his luck. Greek girls of good family were unlikely to be as accommodating.

Damon, however, was different. He was an accident waiting to happen. I thought that I was in love with him. The temptation was great but the circumstances never seemed right. Apart from anything else, we were only allowed out from school for days, not for nights, and the flat in Earl's Court was pretty squalid, not exactly the setting I had in mind.

Then came the Christmas holidays. Damon, who belonged to a fringe branch of a huge aristocratic clan which divided its time between the west coast of Scotland, Ireland and southern England, went home to his family in Argyll. I was with my parents who were over from Greece, staying in the cold, little, grey farmhouse in Berkshire that was our home base (some twenty-five years earlier my father, out riding or walking, had come over the crest of the hill, seen the valley lying below and had decided that this was where he wanted to spend the rest of his life). Every morning, when the postman came, I rushed to the door. Nothing. The days, the weeks, went by, and still I didn't hear from him. I was desperate.

In early January, I went up to London to spend the final week of the holidays with an aunt who lived in Stockwell in south London. I rang Damon as soon as I arrived and he suggested that I come and see him in Camden Town, where he was staying in his mother's mews house. I went that evening, 5th January, 1970. Damon's friend, Johnny, the other Old Etonian, was there and the evening followed the pattern of the Earl's Court days. But with one big difference. This time I stayed the night.

Penetration didn't hurt as much as I had thought it would and afterwards Damon said: 'You can't have been a virgin. You look like a cat that's had the cream.' Gallant as ever. Even through the rose-coloured spectacles of love, this didn't seem quite right.

The next morning I woke in a cloud of happiness. The cloud lasted all of two days. I got up. Damon made breakfast – eggs and bacon. Then I took the bus over to Notting Hill where I met Fleur and told her everything. I told her that Damon and I would get married. But I was wrong. What actually happened was that I didn't see Damon again before I went back to school. I couldn't understand what I had done. Every time Damon and I spoke on the telephone – usually, always in fact, it was me who called him – he would make some excuse about why he couldn't see me. Finally, I got up all my courage and asked him if perhaps he simply didn't want to see me. 'No, no, it's nothing like that,' he said, with a warm, convincing laugh.

But that is just what it was – and for the first and only time in my life (that is, until the death of my father), I lost weight out of sheer misery. School started. I went back there and cried every day and every night until March, when I knew he would be leaving for South America on an eight-month trip with Johnny after which there would be no point in hoping any more.

In the year that had elapsed between sleeping with Damon and meeting Louis, I had learnt a thing or two. I had come to understand that I didn't know how to say 'No', and also that I didn't always want to say 'No'. I had slept with several boys, eager brothers of my school friends. I didn't like *it* much, but I liked *them* too much – just because I had done it with them.

In general, the sexual act left me, not exactly cold, more lukewarm. I liked kissing and the feel of another body against mine and I liked rolling around with my clothes on, but I found naked erections alarming. (I preferred them safely encased in jeans.)

But everyone else was doing it, and I had been locked up in a convent for years and I still thought that if a man wanted to sleep with me, it was something to be grateful for. It wasn't that I was worried that they would ditch me if I said 'No'. It was more that I was pathetically grateful for their desire and failed to recognize its indiscriminate nature.

In late January 1971, just four weeks after I had met Louis, my family left Greece for good. My brother and sister returned to school in England and I went with my mother and father to Italy. We drove to Nauplion and stayed the night in a hotel with a view across the town roofs to the bay. From there we took a boat to Bari, then drove the crooked length of Italy to the Veneto where my parents had built a house. Their intention was to retire there one day, although they never did. My father couldn't bear to be parted from his valley in Berkshire. We were to spend a month in Italy before going home to England.

Louis came to stay with us for a week. I can't remember exactly how this came about or even how we had become such good friends – if indeed we had. I think he came to stay because he adored my father, and my father loved to be adored. Apart from Louis' beauty, my father would have liked his mind: his lively intelligence, his erudition, so rare in one so young, his ability with languages. Louis may well have wanted to sleep with *me*, but it was my father he wanted to talk and listen to.

Ten days before Louis arrived, I had a dream about him. I dreamt that he came to me in my old room in Athens, crying, and knelt, burying his face in my lap while he sobbed.

The first night of his visit we stayed up late after my parents had gone to bed. We were in the drawing-room, sitting together on the dark green, velvet sofa that had belonged to my maternal grandparents. The room, long and light, with French windows that opened on to a stone terrace where we ate in summer and which overlooked the Venetian plain, was lit only by a couple of table lamps. Louis got up to put another log on the fire. When he came back, he sat closer to me, then slid his arm slowly along the back of the sofa, over my shoulders. He pulled me to him. Neither of us, it seemed, had had much practice at kissing. Our lips met – or rather they missed – in the clumsy, nuzzling, affectionate way of the inexperienced. We bumped noses, then adjusted, twisting slightly so that our mouths joined, fitting comfortably together, like two pieces of a jigsaw puzzle.

I closed my eyes. Louis' mouth was warm, his lips felt slightly chapped, his tongue was sweet and moist rather than wet. His skin was as soft as if he barely shaved.

That afternoon we had walked up a nearby hill to look at a beautiful red, Romanesque church. It had been fun. I realized that I was pleased to see him and pleased that he had come to see me. So the kissing was fine. I've always liked kissing. It's how you express tenderness, how you show you care. But then, almost before I knew it, we were embracing on the sofa. Louis was breathing hard as he slid his hand under my sweater, pushed up the soft material and fumbled with the hooks at the back of my bra. Then, it was as if he'd suddenly got the knack, discovered the secret, the magic formula, the combination to the safe, and I felt my bra come loose and his cold hands on my breasts. The hands moved down to the zipper of my jeans and, all the while, there was the insistent, hot weight of his penis to remind me that there was no going back.

Some code of behaviour which endured until I was well into my thirties (together with a belief that it was *physically* painful for men to be denied) dictated to me that what you started, you had to finish. There was no such thing as 'date rape' then. I asked Louis if he was a virgin and, when he said 'Yes', I didn't see that I had any choice. We got up from the sofa and we went into his bedroom, my brother's room, a small, single room, on the ground floor. My parents were asleep upstairs. It was over quickly. I hardly felt a thing but Louis showered appreciative kisses on my face. His gratitude only added to my shame.

But I refused to do it again and, when we took the bus into Venice and shared a room for the night, I insisted on separate beds and I wouldn't let him near me.

After that we would run into each other occasionally and go to bed, though we only once spent a whole night together. Then we wouldn't see each other again for years. In all, we can't have encountered one another more than five or six times in twenty-five years and we slept together on just three occasions, even though, for long periods, we lived in the same city.

Once Louis gave me a gold chain which I subsequently sold when completely broke. On another occasion he telephoned me one night, around midnight, to say that he would kill himself if I wouldn't let him come to see me. I didn't want to see him and I didn't believe that he would kill himself, but I was sufficiently concerned to ring a mutual friend, who suggested that I should call his wife – which is what I did do, and she thanked me politely. When, some time later, I glimpsed him at a party, he whispered in my ear, as he squeezed past me in the crush, 'You betrayed me.'

I heard nothing more from Louis for years. I learnt on the grapevine that he and his wife had parted but I didn't care. It was nothing to do with me, but, when he left a message on my answering-machine on the day of my father's death the coincidence was too great to ignore. Now I thought, finally, we should give it a go, a proper go. Falling in love is, I've always thought, almost entirely a question of timing, and so, in an access of confusion, grief and vulnerability, I fell in love with Louis.

Two

I had found Louis' message asking me to dinner when I rang home from my parents' house on the evening of the day of my father's death. My answering-machine didn't specify the time of the call, but I was convinced that Louis had telephoned me at exactly the moment when my father died. That conviction filled me with a kind of confidence, a belief in fate. It became an article of faith which would override every difficulty, every obstacle that might lie between us. It proved that our reunion had been preordained, that we were meant to be together.

I didn't call him back for a couple of days. It was impossible. There was too much going on. But it was strange: even while I was consumed by emotion and practicalities, I was constantly aware of the phone call that I had to make. That awareness lurked, deep in my subconscious, like a childhood memory, and it comforted me. I knew, as soon as I had got Louis' message, that I would telephone him, that I would see him and that I would sleep with him. The notion that I would marry him even strayed across my mind.

As I drove through the countryside to collect my father's death certificate, as I went with my brother to choose my father's coffin, as I argued with my sister about the choice of hymns, as I endured the funeral service, as I sparkled and shone at the wake – the best party I have ever given – I kept with me the knowledge of the future and this gave me strength.

We had arranged to meet at a cocktail party to which, by coincidence, we had both been invited. I had come down to London from the village in Oxfordshire where I was living. The party, to launch a guide to the Season (the sporting and social season, that is, not the winter, which was shortly to begin), was held in Mayfair in a sporting-goods shop. It was the first time that I had done something social since my father's death and I could hardly have chosen a more bizarre re-entry into the world. The whole occasion seemed surreal. The guide's author was the daughter of a duke – she had fallen on hard times, hence the project, but she could still, it seemed, persuade the cream of the British upper classes to turn out for her. Here they all were, sipping champagne and nibbling smoked-salmon titbits, lounging confidently against glass-fronted cabinets filled with shotguns with chased steel-blue barrels and mahogany stocks. Rails of mud-coloured, waterproofed jackets, mounds of green Wellington boots, heaps of cashmere sweaters and scarves in country greens and browns provided the backdrop to their chatter. Their voices sounded eager and high-pitched, as if they were actually out on the hunting-field, urging on the hounds. Perhaps it was just the effect of sheer numbers. I felt separated from them, as if there were an invisible wall between us. I stood alone to one side; they were on the other side. There was no common ground.

I couldn't see Louis anywhere in the crowd. Looking for him, I came face to face with a friend of my parents, who lived near them in the country. This woman, a former night-club singer and, bizarrely, an ambassadress, had, in late middle-age, embarked on yet another career and decided to train as a psychotherapist. Now, or so it seemed, she thought she would seize the opportunity to try out her newly acquired skills on me.

'I'm so sorry about your father,' she said. 'How do you feel? I mean, do you feel that there was something you wanted to say to him and now you'll never be able to?'

'Please,' I said, 'oh, please, not now, not *here*.' I walked away from her without saying goodbye and, almost immediately, found Louis. He was standing at the foot of the stairs, holding a half-full glass of white wine and looking strained and unhappy. When he saw me, his mouth, which was set and tense as if he were grinding his teeth together, relaxed into a twisted smile. 'For God's sake, let's get out of here,' he said.

In the taxi, he repeated what he had said when we had arranged the rendezvous, 'It's not really my sort of thing.'

'Nor mine,' I answered. 'If a bomb were to drop and kill the lot of them, I'd rejoice.'

He laughed and said, 'You were the prettiest person there.'

The taxi took us to an old-fashioned Greek restaurant in Charlotte Street where Louis had booked a table. I could barely eat. Alcohol – of which, at the time, I was consuming vast quantities – had almost no effect on me. But I do remember that Louis ordered two ouzos at the beginning of dinner. I remember, too, that I merely picked at the food. I remember Louis saying that he wanted to see if he still loved me and I remember saying, 'Well, perhaps we should try to make a go of it, a proper go. What do you think?' and then he nodded, smiling, and said that he felt very happy.

There was no reason to linger and neither of us had been able to eat more than a few mouthfuls. Louis asked for the bill. The old Greek waiter who brought it tut-tutted at the waste, shaking his head, and asked what was wrong with the food. Outside in the street, Louis tried to kiss me under a lamppost and I pushed him away. He didn't seem to mind and we walked along, holding hands, until we found a taxi.

'Where are we going?' I asked, not really caring.

'Back to my place,' he said.

Louis lived in a maisonette at the top of a narrow, white, nineteenth-century stucco house in Kensington. I had never been there before. I had never even known where he lived. His rooms were arranged with a peculiar mixture of care and neglect: the sitting-room was furnished formally, as if it belonged to someone much older. It contained a few good pieces of polished furniture, their patina denoting age and value; a couple of decent oil paintings – one of them, it transpired, the work of an ancestor – and many piles of books, mainly books about English history. There were a few little ornamental *objets* carefully positioned on a side table – a tiny, turquoise reproduction of a hippopotamus from the British Museum; a silver dagger, which looked as if it might be Turkish; the marble head of a young boy; a dandelion-yellow glazed Chinese plate – and these were arranged with care, rather than for artistic effect. A single, large, ugly, comfortable armchair stood directly in front of the television set; its position redolent of long evenings of solitary viewing.

The kitchen sink was full of unwashed dishes; a jar of Nescafé stood open on the counter; a plate with remnants of last night's dinner – fried eggs, by the look of it – still lay on the table, an open book next to it; a bunch of bronze pom-pom chrysanthemums, the kind you always see in Japanese prints, were wilting and rotting in a vase, their big heads drooping like so many rag dolls. The kitchen, indeed the whole apartment, smelt strange, musty and sour, but after a few minutes I ceased to notice this.

All the signs were there, had I been in a fit state to interpret them. This was a lonely person's home, the lair of a frightened, solitary animal, not intended for fun or even for social life.

'There's nothing to drink, I'm afraid,' he said.

'It doesn't matter,' I said, 'I've had enough.'

When, in time, I came to know this place better, it evoked in me a kind of angry pity. I wanted to assuage its isolation. I wanted to kiss it better. I wanted to kiss Louis better.

Louis made two mugs of Earl Grey tea (both mugs were chipped and there was no milk) and we carried them up to the bedroom, a small, pale room under the eaves with a vast double bed. The sheets were fresh and very white. They must have been put on clean that day. Louis had been confident of the evening's outcome. He put his arms around me, began to kiss me, to try to undress me, but I pushed him away. I was moving sluggishly, like a sleepwalker or someone who was drugged. I didn't really know what was happening and it didn't seem to matter. I took off my clothes slowly: first my sweater, tight, black; then my long, black skirt; then, sitting on the edge of the bed, I bent to unzip my black ankle boots and pull them off. I stood up to remove my tights, then I crawled under the duvet in my underclothes. Louis came to lie with me. He was trembling slightly. With fear? With desire? I don't know. He began to caress me cautiously, stroking my arms and back, unfastening my bra, pushing down my pants, until finally I was naked. As he lowered himself on top of me, into me, his slender, muscular body seemed utterly familiar. His skin was very soft and warm, like silk. Like mine. His breath smelt of cigarettes and wine. His penis was smooth and very stiff, as if he had been wanting me for months.

That first night we spent together — two days after my father's funeral — I hardly slept. Around four, I got up and went downstairs to read. I read a detective story by P. D. James which I found in a bookcase on the stairs. I read for several hours — until the grim, grey light of dawn filtered through the gaps in the curtains. It felt like the longest night of my life.

The next morning we left the apartment early. I felt strange and disoriented. Louis kissed me hard on the mouth, said he would telephone later and hurried to catch a bus to work. I walked along the street till I came to a French café. I wasn't hungry but I drank a cup of coffee and glanced at a newspaper. My whole body felt taut and raw, the nerve-endings singing with unappeased desire and lack of sleep. Yet I wasn't tired. I felt as if I had taken cocaine: tense, excited and on the verge of tears, at the beginning of a great adventure.

And, in a way, that's just what it was. But, in my haste to fall in love, to settle down before it was too late, and in the extreme vulnerability of the moment, I discounted reality, the years in between, the broken marriages, the baggage we both now carried. Maybe it would have been all right if we had been younger – now everything seemed to be set in stone. Couples have to learn to be couples when young and I had never been able to learn that lesson.

Three

The next night, alone again in Oxfordshire, I dreamt that I was in an unfinished house or apartment. Electric cables dangled from the walls and the ceiling and the floorboards were all up, revealing the pipes and the wiring beneath. You had to tread carefully on the narrow timbers that were the basic framework of the floor, and on which the floorboards would later be replaced. It was dark – the electricity had been disconnected – and I held a torch, which cast a slender, unsteady beam. Suddenly, shrilly, in another room, the telephone began to ring. I rushed to answer it but, because of the treacherous floor, it took several minutes to reach it. I got there, I felt, just in time. I lifted the receiver and heard my mother's voice.

'Darling,' she said, 'Daddy's killed himself – in a car crash.'

This was only a dream but in real life, too, this kind of melodramatic display was typical of my mother. Even on an occasion already fraught with drama, she could never resist the chance to dramatize further. On a different night I had dreamt that my mother had sent my father away to die on his own; yet another time, that I accompanied her to his funeral and that he was there, at his own funeral, looking thin and old.

In fact, every morning since his death I had woken either at dawn, or just before it, with a sensation of loss and dread. And I hated this. It made the days so long. It made the beginning of the day so bleak. It made me so tired. My father had died at home in his bed and I had been there. That sounds better than it actually was. I cannot bear to remember his face in those last hours. I had gone to my parents' house for Sunday lunch. When I had arrived, the stove was cold; the food unprepared; the table unlaid, and my mother was upstairs with my father. He had not been well for some time. He didn't have cancer or heart disease but he had all sorts of other things, little things. Since a riding accident and since his retirement, his body had been wearing out. There is a line in the funeral service about the burden of the flesh. His flesh had become a burden.

Just over a year before, our old nanny, the woman who had looked after us when we were children, had also died. I had been sitting at her bedside in hospital when it happened. She had looked terrible, all the flesh drained away from her bones. I don't know the exact moment when the breath, the spirit, when *life* left her body – I was talking to the nurse – but, in retrospect, it seems as if a cool wind had entered the room.

When I saw my father that Sunday, I recognized that he looked rather as Nanny had looked just before she died. And I was right. He died within hours. Not in pain – the young locum who came gave him morphine and told me that there was nothing to be done – not in distress, but without those final words of comfort and love and farewell that my mother would so much have liked to hear from him. She kept saying so. I told her that only happened in the movies, that the perfect death was almost certainly an illusion.

A few days after our affair began, Louis came to see me at my parents' house where I was engaged in the melancholy task of sorting through my dead father's clothes. My mother had gone to stay with her sister. It was the first time since the funeral that I had been back to the house. After she drove off, I went upstairs and began to open drawers and cupboards.

My father had had so many clothes. Some of them I had had made for him while I was travelling in the Far East: from Hong Kong, shirts and special, colonial-style bush jackets with epaulettes and belts and pockets with flaps. Then there were the sarongs that I had bought for him in Bangkok or Penang. He had acquired a taste for these when living in the East and would wear them to sleep in instead of pyjamas. As he grew older, he would lounge around the house in a sarong, pyjama jacket and cashmere waistcoat with a silk scarf round his neck, looking simultaneously dashing and vaguely seedy. There they were: piles of silk handkerchiefs, sarongs in the random batiks of the East, shirts, cashmere jerseys, many with little holes as if mice had been nesting in them, baggy old worn underpants, string vests. I felt their presence like a reproach and bundled them into plastic bags for the local charity shop, even though half of them should just have been consigned to the dustbin.

My father, like his father and grandfather, both of them civil servants, had been born in India. If his father, my grandfather, hadn't died, from cancer and overwork, leaving his wife a widow with seven children at the age of thirty-seven, he might well have made his life in India too. But after my grandfather's death, the family came back to England and settled in Sussex. When my grandfather died, my father was only nine; blond, blue-eyed, deaf in one ear from measles, he was the darling of his sisters, who favoured him over his elder brother, Gerald, whom he resembled closely. (As they grew up, my uncle, who had a brief career in the Indian Army Cavalry and then never worked again after the age of thirty-five, came more and more to appear the pale imitation of his vibrant, better-looking, younger brother.)

Like almost every boy of his class at that time, my father was sent to boarding-school, then up to Cambridge. While at Cambridge, he travelled. When he left – before taking a degree – he moved to Rome, to paint. He thought that he wasn't good enough to make a career out of art (by his exacting standards, I'm sure he was right), so, after a brief spell in a museum attending to the needs of valuable porcelain, he joined the Foreign Service, and from then on he was constantly on the move. Rome, Lisbon, Singapore, Ankara, Peking, Washington, Athens, with myriad side trips to Madrid, Kuala Lumpur, Istanbul, Tehran, Saigon, Phnom Penh, Bangkok, Ulan Bator, Beirut, New York, Nicosia, Virginia, Venice – his life flashed before his family like a revolving globe. Diplomat as whirling dervish.

Even when he retired, he was torn between a life in Italy or in England, then ended up shuttling between London and the country.

The house in which my parents lived was one which they had built from scratch on a plot of land, barely more than an acre, which they had bought from my aunt. They had done this after the owner of the small farmhouse in the valley with which my father had fallen in love as a young man announced that he was arbitrarily revising the terms of the lease. The new terms would enable him, in the event of my father's death, to throw my mother out with three months' notice. My mother had never cared much for the farmhouse anyway; she resented the money they had poured into it over the years and she disliked its red-faced owner. This latest development was the last straw, and they moved a mere quarter of a mile away, to a house which my father designed.

The new house was more spacious and more elegant, but we children still had to share rooms as we had done when we were small and spent our holidays in the farmhouse up the road. The new house started out as a rectangle (there was a big living/dining-room downstairs and two bedrooms, my parents' bedroom and another which my father used as a dressing-room, and a bathroom upstairs) with a square tower at one end, which contained the spare bedroom and the kitchen. My parents then added another bathroom off the main bedroom, so they could each have a bathroom, then a study at the end of the drawing-room. The next additions were a kind of lean-to off the kitchen which housed a chest freezer and the gumboots, and a library, where my father kept his books, his clothes and a piano. Then, some years later, another bedroom (for the grandchildren) appeared; it sat on top of a vast, new utility room, which opened off the drawing-room. The result of all this building was that, though the front of the house looked quite neat and tidy, the back seemed a higgledy-piggledy jumble and inside was a rabbit warren of odd little rooms.

It had always been difficult for me to think of that house as home. Now that my father was dead, it was impossible. It had been their house, their home, not mine. For one thing, it wasn't big enough to accommodate the whole family at any one time, or at least not at the level of comfort to which we had become accustomed. Although they kept adding on rooms, there were still not enough bedrooms and those that there were varied in size and comfort, so one of us always drew the short straw. In reality, this didn't matter because the likelihood of us all being there at the same time was remote but, in all our minds, there was always a conflict between my mother's demand that we come 'home' and our difficulty in thinking of a house in which we had no place as 'home'.

After a day sorting through my father's clothes I drove to the small local railway station to meet Louis off the evening train from London. The station was little used; a couple of trains came in the morning and again in the evening, and the ticket office was often left unmanned. There was just a single track spanned by a bridge, so there was never more than one train at a time standing in the station. I sat on a bench on the platform and waited.

My affair with Louis was still in the intense, early stages, when everything felt both passionate and detached – almost cinematic, as if we were operating in slow motion. Everything seemed to have a significance, a weight, far beyond any that it could actually have. Ever since my father died, ever since I fell in love, everything, even the most mundane everyday actions, was – or appeared to be – suffused with meaning.

I sat at the foot of the bridge, smoking a cigarette. I was wearing a long, black skirt, a low-necked, black jersey and black stockings, leopardskin-printed ankle boots, and a big, loose, expensive, Italian raincoat. My hair was clean and soft and shiny and I had painted my mouth with a dark, fuschia-red St Laurent lipstick. I sat, like a Forties film star, under the single light that illuminated the platform and waited.

When the London train arrives at that station, passengers get off on the far platform and then cross over the bridge to go out of the station. The first you see of them is their shoes and then their legs as they come down the steps from the bridge. When I saw my lover's legs, I looked down, partly in shyness, partly because I wanted him to see what a great picture I made.

It was a brilliant, crisp, starry night, cold and clear. There was a tape in the machine in the car, one that I had made for another lover – in another life – and I punched it in. The sweet tones of Connie Francis filled the car. She was singing a song called 'Tennessee Waltz', which my mother used to sing to me as a child. God knows why. It isn't exactly a lullaby.

> I was waltzing with my darling to the Tennessee Waltz
> When an old friend I happened to see
> Introduced her to my loved one
> And while they were waltzing
> My friend stole my sweetheart from me.

As we came down the hill from the gibbet where once men had been hung for stealing, the song ended, and

Juliette Greco began to sing 'Parlez-moi d'amour'. We were both almost paralysed by shyness. Back at my parents' house we circled around each other for a while, like dogs marking territory. It was the first time that we had seen each other since that first night in London and, though I was nearly fainting with desire – and, I imagine, he was too – I couldn't make a move. Eventually Louis said, 'Is it OK if I have a bath?' and took himself off upstairs. I sat and watched television. I remember that the programme was one I very much wanted to watch, but I can't, for the life of me, recall what it was. Then I cooked dinner – roast partridge with lentils and sauté potatoes.

That evening Louis taught me that, if you add a little water to the pan, the potatoes don't burn – they do, however, go soggy. I had never, in a long career of romances as well as a marriage, been to a supermarket with a man. (I used to look at those couples on Saturday mornings, selecting pasta, out-of-season vegetables and legs of lamb, in amazement, as if I was watching Martians.) But such culinary skills as I possessed I had learnt from men. Useful solid lessons in the basics.

One lover taught me how to make a perfect omelette (you can only do it right if you have the right frying pan – an iron, that is, steel, one; non-stick is hopeless) and how to poach fish. Another simply infused me with a passion for cooking. One of the happiest days of my life was spent cooking Christmas lunch with him in Ireland. Every plate in his kitchen was chipped. His legacy was a passion for recipe books. I read them as if they are detective stories.

Women always learn *things* from men (one man who

had lived in Japan taught me that you must trim cut flowers under *running* water – the flowers take a desperate gulp when they are snipped, you must let them drink; another taught me how make a perfect margarita: one third tequila, one third Cointreau, one third fresh lime juice. Facts, skills, statistics, never wisdom. Men are great teachers. They know it all.

After dinner, we began to make love. We began on the floor in front of the fire, then moved to the sofa. Desire shimmered between us like a heat haze.

Louis said, 'I am happier now than I will ever be.'

'Why do you say that?' I asked. 'I'm not going to leave you. I'll be here.'

'Your skin smells like burnt toast and honey,' he said. 'Don't ever wash. I want you always to smell like this.'

Later, as we lay upstairs in my parents' bed, he said, 'We'll be together for ever. We're like the stones at Mycenae, so close that not even the blade of a knife could come between us.'

'I love you,' I said. I believed what I was saying.

'No', he said. 'Don't get keen on me. I'm not worth it.' That was what he *said*. But he wanted me to contradict him and I did.

That night and the first night, the one after my father's funeral, I will remember till I die. But he knew more than I did. In the pure, shining light of passion, he knew himself, and perhaps he knew me, better than I thought.

Four

Four years after we first slept together in Italy, Louis and I met again in Oxford. Then, later on Valentine's Day, we bumped into each other in a pub. After many drinks, we reeled back to my single bed in the house where my brother and sister lived. We were both smashed enough to claim, had we been questioned in the cold, clear light of day, that we didn't know what we were doing. But, as my every encounter with Louis *seemed* significant (if not at the time, then retrospectively), even when its significance wasn't apparent, that night had a momentous quality, enhanced no doubt by the drink.

Louis was making quite a splash in university society. He was young for his year, having won a scholarship, and, as one girl put it, he was desperately handsome. This was an apt phrase; there was something *desperate* about his handsomeness. Something wild-eyed and Byronic. The pure beauty of his teens, when he had looked like a chorister or an angel, had matured; debauchery had given him an additional, sexual, charge. He was drinking and taking drugs – speed, cocaine, marijuana, heroin even – with wild abandon, but then so was everyone else.

In Oxford, Louis had a girlfriend called Anna. Tall, long legs, tawny hair and big blue eyes. She had a sweet face and – as far as I could tell – a sweet character to match. I barely knew her. She wasn't at the university; she attended one of the smart secretarial-colleges-cum-finishing-schools with which Oxford was littered. You weren't expected to learn much at these establishments; rather the idea was that young women of good family would meet and subsequently marry young men with prospects. The girls were training to be wives under the guise of acquiring qualifications, qualifications that would eventually help them to get a poorly paid job in London, perhaps as a receptionist in a fashionable art gallery, or as personal assistant to a smart publisher, or to sit behind the front desk at Sotheby's or Christie's, while they waited for marriage and motherhood. People said that Louis and Anna were *terribly* in love; indeed they seemed always to be together, an apparently golden couple.

But he still wanted me – or wanted me to want him. When he drawled, 'Let's go back to your place, darling,' I asked him, 'Why? Why do you want to sleep with me?' He answered, 'Well, you see, da-a-arling, I suppose I really rather love you.' It was very sweet but so obviously phoney that it was frightening. I wanted to believe him but I didn't, not for a minute; it wasn't love that he felt; it was more like an itch that needed to be scratched.

At some point, in the middle of that night, Louis had forgotten about love and was saying, 'Darling, you're such a good fuck' as he thrust into me. Well, I wanted to be a good fuck. All my girlfriends did, as well. We dreamed of being sexually expert, conversant with the teachings and techniques of the Kama Sutra, as alluring as Mata Hari, yet simultaneously winsome and innocent like little Bo Peep. It was an ambition for which our education had prepared us, but when Louis actually put it into these words, I found that I preferred him to tell me that he loved me.

Maybe I am misjudging Louis. Perhaps he did love me then. Perhaps he always had, just as he claimed, and my initial rejection of him, like Damon's rejection of me, had set in motion a train of events and emotions that were to dog us all for the rest of our days.

The next morning I was sober and ashamed. My brother and sister had heard us screwing – I use this word deliberately – and hadn't relished the experience. I gave Louis a lift to the station; he was going to the Lake District to visit his mother. He wrote to me from there asking that I send him a photograph of myself. So I did, but didn't hear another word from him.

It was almost eight years since I had last slept with Louis. Our third encounter had taken place at my old flat in Notting Hill Gate during the chaotic, promiscuous aftermath of the break-up of my marriage. Louis' wife was in hospital recovering from an operation to remove her appendix. Two nights of frenzied sex had sated, drained and somewhat disgusted me; a week later, when he rang my doorbell, I wouldn't let him in.

But now I was almost forty-two and apparently no nearer to finding happiness or love, let alone the two together. It was too late. I was, I felt, too old. In the intervening years I had had a number of lovers (we are talking double figures) and considered myself to have been in love three times. I was always looking to fall in love, to *be* in love. I wanted a great love, my life's companion, a comrade-in-arms, someone with whom I could metaphorically, if not literally, climb mountains.

There had been a number of false starts, times when I had thought, 'This is it'. Then it turned out it wasn't it. Sometimes the beloved object didn't measure up, was found unexpectedly wanting in some small but vitally important way. It's a subtle thing – they have to give but not too much. Sometimes time and distance have intervened, imposing restrictions which I only became aware of afterwards, when it was too late. There's no point in choosing a great love who lives three thousand miles away and who assumes that those miles dictate the nature of the relationship.

And sex, even bad sex, always muddies the waters. It's not called 'making love' for nothing and I have yet to learn to tell the difference between sexual pleasure and the pleasure of being made love to.

But I measure being in love by the amount of pain I experience. True love is, by definition, unrequited.

Although this was the most telling occasion, it was not the first time that I had been given another chance with a man. I once had a lover with whom I had three – three! – unsuccessful 'affairettes'. Then, some fifteen years later, after he had married, when his marriage had begun to grow stale and formal, we got together again secretly and wondered why *now* we could get on as never before. He thought that it was because I had changed.

So, now, did Louis, who said: 'Darling, you used to be so-o-o difficult.' I wasn't difficult before. I just knew less, needed less and wanted more. Now, particularly now, I recognized my limitations and was grateful for what I could get.

'Some pleasure is too much like pain,' I said to Louis

as we made love early one evening. With him, it was never just my body that was naked. This time round I was the virgin, exposed, completely raw, peeled as if he could see into my heart and soul. (This was another illusion: what he saw was me aged eighteen and not rebuffing him. The bit of the illusion that *I* welcomed was the idea of being eighteen again. Inside I was eighteen. The song goes, 'I'm gonna be eighteen till I die . . .' I wasn't going to argue.)

'That will be the first line of your novel,' he said.

Later that evening we went for dinner in a tiny Malay restaurant and, holding hands across the table, began talking about Lampedusa's *The Leopard*.

'Do you remember the chapter when Tancredi and Angelica play hide-and-seek in the forgotten rooms at Donnafugata?' I asked.

He nodded and said, 'Incandescent with lust.'

I smiled.

'Like us,' he added.

(Later, much later, I looked up that section of the book; it ended with the words 'Those days were the preparation for a marriage which, even erotically, was no success; a preparation, however, in a way sufficient to itself, exquisite and brief; like those overtures which outlive the forgotten operas they belong to and hint in delicate veiled gaiety at all the arias which later in the opera are to be developed undeftly, and fail.')

Another time, I told him about my favourite film, *The Year of Living Dangerously*, a story of love and danger and war set in Sukarno's Indonesia.

'Just like us,' he said.

'Without the war,' I said.

We were in love with being in love, as if we were very young, rather than on the verge of middle-age.

One evening, after Louis and I had been sleeping together for some weeks, he called me. He sounded agitated.

'Hello, darling, what's up?' I said. 'Did you have a good weekend?'

'It's Sara. She knows about us.'

'Is that so terrible?' I asked. 'You would have had to tell her anyhow.'

There was a silence, then Louis said, 'Well, it's a little more complicated than that.'

Why am I not surprised?

'I'm afraid I wasn't entirely truthful with you.'

Sara was Louis' girlfriend. I already knew that. At dinner in Charlotte Street that first night, I had asked him if he had a girlfriend. 'Yes,' he answered. I would have been amazed if he hadn't. He always had a girl-friend. He had to. It was as natural to him as breathing, as certain as sunrise. I asked him what he would do about Sara if things worked out between us. 'I'll give her her congé,' he said. The brutality with which he had spoken only struck me in retrospect.

When Louis picked up the phone to call me late that Sunday afternoon as I sat beside my dying father's bedside, he had just returned from spending the weekend with Sara. He had been thinking, he later told me, about telephoning me for some time; the weekend, which had been difficult and quarrelsome, decided him. He hadn't, however, thought beyond the call; he hadn't considered what an involvement with me might mean. Perhaps he thought that what had always happened in the past – an intense encounter, then nothing – would inevitably occur again. In any event, neither of us was prepared for what did happen, that this time, because of the peculiar circumstances in which I found myself, we would embark on a full-scale, passionate affair.

Louis and Sara had been together for almost five years. They spent a couple of evenings a week, weekends and holidays together. At weekends they went to the country, to a cottage which Louis rented in the hills near Salisbury. On the nights when they weren't with each other, Louis would telephone Sara last thing, just before he went to bed. They had a life together; they were a couple. They might as well have been married; they just didn't happen to have any children. Sara adored Louis (or so he said); she thought him handsome (*très beau*, as Louis put it, as if the French would remove any taint of hubris) and intelligent. She didn't want to lose him. And, naturally, she was not at all happy when she discovered that Louis had been unfaithful to her, though I doubt it was the first time. Louis said that he didn't know how she had found out – he assumed that someone had seen us (when I stopped to think about this, it seemed highly unlikely: we hardly ever got out of bed when we were together). She was, Louis told me with panic-stricken surprise, threatening to leave him and, much as he wanted me, the prospect of losing her terrified him.

I don't know much about couple life. My experience of it has been limited. It is true that I have been married but it wasn't for very long and I am used to being alone. In the past, when I was younger and more reckless, I had two long affairs with married men. I had, it seemed, what amounted to a moral blind spot. I could never see that it was wrong to sleep with married men. I wasn't trying to get the man to leave his wife; and in neither case did I break up the marriage, though the men in question had loved me very much and had pursued me.

In many ways, these affairs suited me very well – for a while. I liked the intrigue, the theatre of it all; I liked being visited for what the French term *un cinq à sept*, that interlude between five and seven in the afternoon, when men have left the office for the day and before they have to go home to their wives. I liked meeting my lover for lunch in a fancy restaurant, then spending the afternoon making love as the evening drew in. I even enjoyed his departure. I liked standing at the top of the stairs in a silk dressing gown, to say goodbye, then closing the door and being alone in my flat. I was content to sleep alone, sated, the memory of the afternoon imprinted on my flesh. I felt loved and secure – secure enough to accommodate the situation. The long afternoons I spent in bed with Louis, drinking champagne and making love, evoked for me an earlier, happier time, when the present and the future hadn't seemed so bleak. I suppose I thought, if I thought about it at all, that we would simply continue as we were.

It has taken me years to understand that I don't want domesticity. I have never really wanted it. I had a go at it, when I was barely twenty and then again when I was married but it never took. I crave solitude. But Louis was surprisingly conventional. He wanted a house, a home, a family, professional success, a loving wife. He wasn't a bohemian at all. He said to me more than once, 'The trouble is, I'm too straight for you'.

The first time he said this, I thought, 'You, too straight? What a joke,' but I came to see that he was right. There's a song called 'Speed of the Sound of Loneliness', sung by Nanci Griffith. It goes,

> You come home late
> And you come home early
> You come on big
> When you're feeling small
> You come home straight
> And you come home curly
> Sometimes you don't come home at all.
>
> So what in the world's come over you?
> What in heaven's name have you done?
> You've broken the speed of the sound of loneliness
> You're out there runnin'
> Just to be on the run . . .

Every time I hear that song, I think of Louis, straight and curly.

Sara came from a wealthy Roman Catholic family and had a job as a cataloguer with an art gallery in Mayfair. She was a couple of years older than Louis and had never been married. I didn't know her and didn't know anyone else who knew her. Louis wouldn't tell me what she looked like – he said only, 'She's not a beauty like you' – but I guessed that she must be pretty enough. Initially, it had been difficult to think of her as a real person, impossible to regard her as a threat, when, in conversation,

Louis dismissed her so casually. But now here she was in my life, an unexpected, unwelcome complication. That sounds cold, but it was how I felt. Whatever else might go wrong between us, whatever dangers the future held, I believed that Louis loved me. And, that being the case, he couldn't love anyone else (he told me that he had never pretended to love Sara, never used what he termed the 'L' word to her) and therefore it was only a matter of time. After all, hadn't Louis told me that he would get rid of her? It is, or was, a measure of my naïvety that I still believed that love conquered all.

But nothing is ever simple. I couldn't understand why Louis didn't just tell Sara that he loved me and finish with her. He rarely spoke well of her; he despised her, while recognizing that she provided something he needed. He despised himself for needing her and he despised her for filling that need. Nevertheless he didn't want to lose what he had with her; he didn't want to lose the comforting routine of their county life and was, it seemed, so scared at the prospect of change and upheaval, of angry, tearful scenes that he would, I think, have been prepared to break with me. And, of course, he still wasn't being entirely truthful with me.

I wouldn't let him go. I didn't see why I should just bow out gracefully. I was determined to have my chance. Louis shouldn't have wooed and won me two days after my father's funeral.

Because I lived some distance from London and was infrequently in the city, Sara's discovery made no immediate difference to us. Louis, I suspected, made Sara all manner of promises – vowing fidelity, perpetuity, undying love, for all I knew – and we continued otherwise much as before, seeing each other in the afternoons if I was in town and talking on the telephone. Twice, when I rang Louis' flat in London, Louis pretended that my call was a wrong number and I realized that Sara was there. I didn't really mind. My earlier training with married men came back to me and I adjusted quickly to the necessary small constraints. I had always been a better mistress than a wife.

It's strange to get to know a person at one remove. Sara wasn't like me; that much I could tell. She didn't go in for fussing and fiddling around the house. She had not left her mark on his apartment; there were no small, feminine touches, neither in the flat nor even in the house in the country (as I discovered when I eventually went there). Louis said, 'She's not like you. She's not a real chick.'

I wasn't sure what a real chick was in Louis' eyes. Someone who cooked, cleaned up and expressed an interest in interior décor? Someone, perhaps, who wanted to be married and have children? Louis claimed that he had asked Sara to marry him just days after they got together. Her response, he said, had simply been to laugh. Maybe so, but now it seemed clear that she was desperately in love with him. However, so was I, and I was not prepared to give him up.

None the less, I couldn't hate her. I felt sorry for her. I even admired her spirit. I was on her side, really. I grew familiar with her handwriting – bold and spiky – from her letters which Louis left lying around and which I could not resist reading. She wrote in black ink. The relationship which she depicted in these miserable, passionate letters and wished to preserve, bore little relation to the one that Louis described.

Then one day I found a photograph of her in a drawer. She was tall and had dark hair in a bob with a fringe. She was wearing a long, full, flowered skirt and a t-shirt with a low, round neck. There was a deep valley between her breasts. She had a pretty smile with even, white teeth. In her ears she wore big, round gold hoops which made her look like a gypsy and she was dancing in a circle, holding hands with the person on each side. Somewhere in the country, at a summer fair perhaps. She looked happy and relaxed. I wondered when the picture was taken, whether it was recent and, if so, whether Louis was playing some other game I knew nothing about.

Five

At the time of his death and for many years before it, my father and I had an uneasy, unresolved relationship. It was a part of family myth, which neither of us stopped to examine, that he and I didn't get on. I still don't understand the reasons for it, or even how our estrangement came about, except that, when I was eleven or twelve, I stopped wanting to sit on his lap. I no longer wanted him to touch me. If he came to tickle me with his long, bony fingers, I ran screaming to my mother's arms (later, I stopped wanting physical contact with her too). But it wasn't that my father had *done* anything. The change was in me. I was growing up. And, perhaps as a result, he slowly withdrew from me.

It took a while, it didn't happen overnight, but undoubtedly there came a point when I ceased effectively to have two parents, when I had become our mother's child (in time, my sister became our father's daughter – my brother was left to Nanny). This state of affairs continued. By the time I realized what had happened, what my father had let happen – possibly through carelessness or indifference or from a desire to see my mother happy – it was too late.

I date my real troubles with my parents to puberty, that dangerous, wild time, when children want to run away from home – or at least to go out exploring. Instead of taking it in her stride and viewing it as predictable, *normal* and dull, my mother found my teenage obsession with boys distasteful. She began to describe me (to my face) as a 'nymphomaniac' even before I had slept with anyone. I still don't know what my father thought about it all, only what my mother has told me that he thought. She has told me – often – along with other 'home truths', that he hated my apparent promiscuity and disliked me for it. 'Daddy doesn't like you because he thinks you sleep with everybody.'

But on the rare occasions we were alone, my father made an effort to understand me and my generation, even going so far as to listen to *Tommy* and to the Beatles, before pronouncing them 'banal'. As he detested all popular music, even that enjoyed by his own contemporaries, his verdict came as no surprise to me, though I was touched that he had made the effort to listen.

Physically, my father and I resembled each other closely. We were both very fair and had strong features, though my eyes are a sort of greeny-brown while his were blue. I've never felt safe with a man with blue eyes; yet, as an adult, I only was really interested in men who more or less resembled my father. (Louis, with his thick, crisp, brown hair and hazel eyes, was an exception – an aberration.) My mother, with her dark hair (now snow-white), dark eyes and cheekbones like Fanny Ardant's, was a different type. Her great-grandmother had been an Indian woman, from Madras. My mother's moody colouring was her legacy. My ex-husband once told me that it was because my father and I were so alike – and not just to look at – that he didn't like me.

But I am not convinced that my father ever really wanted children. My mother told me that he was impatient with my brother who, she said, cried easily and, poor baby, didn't talk until he was two, because every time he opened his mouth, I pushed him over. She says he was jealous, jealous of anything that took her attention away from him, but sometimes I wonder if, in fact, it was she who was the jealous one, wanting all *his* attention and all *our* attention too. Of the pair of them, she was, and remains, the insecure one.

I've heard it said that children who move house a lot when small remember little of their early lives. This is true enough in my case. I can recall almost nothing, or at least no whole sequences, only fragments of a memory, snapshots. Such memories as I do have are provoked, or possibly sometimes even created, by photographs. I have a picture of my father and I together in Turkey. I must have been five or so and I am riding in front of him on his horse, grasping the pommel of the saddle while he holds on to me, but I've no recollection of the event (though it must have happened more than once), nor can I remember how it felt to have his arms around my waist.

I remember best the years in Peking and, when I try to reassemble the jigsaw puzzle of my childhood, I think that everything was pretty good then. We children were at home, attending a convent day school within bicycling distance of our house. We came back from school for lunch every day and my studies went spectacularly well most weeks; I won a silver shield for outstanding academic performance. As many of my classmates were from countries other than England (only the Russian children went to a different school), and lessons were in

English, I may well have had an unfair advantage.

Nanny and a Chinese *amah* called Soo-Chin cared for us; Soo-Chin would sit on the end of my bed every night until I fell asleep. In my mind's eye I can see her still, in her uniform of white shirt and black trousers, her black hair tied back in a long pigtail, just visible in the dim light that filtered through from the passage. Meanwhile, our parents gave tennis and cocktail parties. There weren't many Western diplomats and they were all pretty much in one another's pockets. Life in the late Fifties hadn't changed much from the kind of social to-ing and fro-ing that I'd read about in novels of diplomatic life in Peking in the Thirties. Unmarried women expected to find (and *did* find) husbands. Nanny could have done so if she had wished. She was pretty, with delicate, slender ankles. My father, in his official capacity, and in the absence of anyone else, officiated at the weddings – like the captain of a ship. I was always the bridesmaid.

In the summer, when the city was stiflingly hot, we went to the seaside and in the winter we skated on the frozen lake in front of the Summer Palace and picnicked in the grounds of the Ming Tombs. There are lots of photographs of these times: of my sister, then still a toddler, swaddled in her padded clothes, ready to go out on the ice; of my brother who always has a sweet, hopeful expression like that of an eager puppy, usually wearing a hat with ear-flaps, which increases the canine resemblance; of myself just beginning to be toothy and self-conscious. This is especially true in one photo, taken at the beach, where my long hair has been tied up in a knot on top of my head: I am looking down sideways at my long, skinny body as if I'm not sure it belongs to me.

Of course, it's easy to read things into photographs, things which you come to know about later. But that particular picture triggers another memory. A real memory of which no photographs exist. Children, Freud says, are sexual beings and I certainly was. I had boyfriends at the time – at school – and I used to bring them home to play. In the game that we played we would push a chair or a chest against my bedroom door, then lie on my bed, pressed tight, tight, up against each other, kissing, enjoying the feeling, pretending to be grown-ups (a girl at school had told me the facts of life – I hadn't found them surprising or repellent) while my brother and sister tried to open the door. Our last summer in China, when I was nine, I had an older boyfriend, a Yugoslav boy of thirteen. One day, on my way between the house and the sea, he caught me and kissed me. I bet it was just after that kiss that the photograph was taken. And I wonder if the overt sexuality in it which is so obvious to me now was obvious to my parents then – obvious and disturbing.

One other photograph from that period tells a story. The picture shows the three of us children sitting outside our house in Peking. We are each perched on separate small, square suitcases – presumably cases in which we had packed our treasures – waiting to leave, to move on. We are dressed formally in velvet-collared, identical coats and my sister and I are wearing hats. These are the clothes of departure.

The degree to which we all regarded China as an especially happy time can be judged by a squabble I had with my sister – after we had grown up and were some twenty years out of childhood – over a photograph album. My mother had a tiny Minox camera in China, no more than an inch wide and three or four inches long; a spy's camera, with which she photographed the country, its people and her own children. Many of these pictures, particularly the ones of us, ended up in a fat album with a cover of padded Chinese silk, painted with a misty landscape of willow tress and little hump-backed bridges. I had the album. One evening I wanted to show it a friend ('See, look what happy, glowing children we were, look how pretty I was when I was small, look how little I have changed') but I couldn't find it anywhere. I drove myself nearly crazy searching for it – its loss was unendurable. There was something talismanic about the album. It was proof that we were once a happy family.

My sister had taken the album. It was her proof too. She denied that she had taken it, but I knew she had. One day, months later, when she thought that I had forgotten all about it, or perhaps had forgotten about it herself, she lent me the keys to her flat so that I could collect a dress or a pair of shoes. I went there, looked for the album – I really had to hunt for it – found it hidden at the back of a cupboard and reappropriated it. Then, one evening, she wanted to show it to someone ('Look, see how happy we were. Wasn't I sweet when I was little?') and, of course, it wasn't there. She was furious. The fact that *she* had taken it from *me* in the first place was irrelevant. The quarrel went on for months, until one morning I woke up, realized that I didn't care any more and let her have it.

The day after my father died I had left the house in the valley in the late afternoon, wearily driven fifty or so miles to the village where I lived, fed my cats, made some calls, collected some clean clothes, arranged for my cleaning lady to feed the cats and drove back in time to cook supper for my mother.

After supper I went to sit in a big, low, rather beautiful, not very comfortable armchair by the fire. My mother, in my memory, is sitting almost at my feet, possibly on a small, round, green velvet footstool that had belonged to her mother. She is understandably weepy and is holding both my hands in hers. Suddenly, she said – it seemed *à propos* of nothing in particular, certainly of nothing remotely relevant – 'The reason that Daddy didn't like you was because you have become so enormously fat'.

I looked at her in amazement, in complete horror. What had I done to deserve this? I wanted to hit her. Instead I said, as calmly as I was able, 'Mummy, please, I'm sure you don't want to have this conversation *now*.'

As if I hadn't spoken, she continued inexorably, 'He *adored* you. When you were a baby, he absolutely *adored* you. He thought you were so beautiful. But then you got so enormously fat; it made him incredibly sad.'

Desperately, as she talked, repeating the same cruel words over and over again, in an unruffled monotone, as though what she was saying was perfectly reasonable, I was saying, 'Please, please, stop it. Not now, not *today*.' But she wouldn't stop, she wouldn't shut up, and eventually I got up and left the room.

I dragged myself upstairs to my parents' room, the room where my father had died, where I was now sleeping. My mother had moved in with my sister, to the double bed in the guest room. I was sleeping alone, on my mother's side of my parents' bed. Even before that evening, I don't think that I could have shared a bed with my mother – yet when I was a child, to do so was my idea of the biggest treat in the world.

The first night I stretched out my hand to where my father would normally have lain. It was a gesture such as one might make to a lover, reassuring, affectionate, a gesture saying 'Hello, I am here. Where are you? Are you there?' That night, on the bed, I curled up in a foetal ball, wrapped in an old paisley dressing gown of my father's. It smelt of him, of sickness and age and a lime hair potion from Trumper's. I put my hand out to the empty side of the bed and whispered, 'Is it true? Is that how you felt?'

My mother had dealt me a terrible blow. Perhaps it was her way of making herself feel better.

Later, just before she went to bed with my sister, she came into the bedroom. I got up off the bed and she attempted to take me in her arms. 'Darling, I love you just the way you are,' she said, in a smooth, caressing voice. I knew my sister had told her to come and see me. I stood stiffly in her embrace.

For the record, I was not, and am not, 'enormously fat' (though it's been a few years since I chose to wear a bikini). From being a skinny child and a slender teenager with late periods, I had retained well into my twenties the long, slim legs, the small, high, rounded breasts, like little apples, and the barely convex stomach of a woman in a Cranach painting. Then, around twenty-seven, I developed a woman's body. Renoir, or perhaps Rubens. What admirers would call voluptuous. It certainly wasn't girlish any more. I had never had any problem in attracting men, and this didn't change, but my mother hated my new shape and told me so. More than once.

Now that I am over forty, I am certainly heavier – fatter, if you insist – than I was at thirty or even at thirty-five.

But I am not 'enormously fat'. And I am still good-looking, I think, though no longer the beauty I was.

Ever since I was a little girl, I've been told that I am beautiful. Not pretty, more than pretty. Beautiful. There are few absolute standards of beauty. That's why we are told that it's in the eye of the beholder. But, by many standards – or the standards of many people – I am, or was, a beauty. Painters have wanted to paint me; photographers to photograph me; men to sleep with me. I've been told that I am beautiful so often that, though I can recognize – and mind about – my defects (crooked teeth, wide hips, bitten nails, ankles that should be slimmer), I have come, in a way, to believe it. I can see my own beauty, especially when I look at pictures of my younger self.

Now I'm losing that beauty. At night, when I'm lying in bed, I sometimes pick up a hand mirror and look at my face. When I'm lying flat, the flesh draws back and the bones are revealed. I still look pretty good. *I think*. But I can tell it's no longer the same. It's not just the coarsened skin, the beginnings of a double chin, the little, brown patches on my face and hands, and the fine lines around my eyes (I don't mind those), but that I no longer look young or fresh. Gravity is winning. And below my nose and to the right, I have a line about half an inch long running down to my lips. I can remember when that line first appeared. It was at that moment that I knew I would grow old, that I was already growing old.

It was in November, four years ago, the year before my father died. I was in the Caribbean where I had gone to visit a man whom I thought I loved. Then the line only manifested itself in the mornings, when I woke up; something about the way I had slept pushed my face together and made the line visible. As the day wore on and my face settled, the line would disappear. I tried smiling a lot to iron out the crease. I put anti-wrinkle cream on it, Retinol A, but it didn't do any good. I knew then that the day would come when the line would be there all the time.

Our faces reflect our characters, our lives. But what frightens me is that I don't feel that I have anything to replace my beauty. Nothing prepared me for its loss (probably nothing prepares anybody for this sort of loss – or for getting fat), perhaps because it never brought me what it promised: love, happiness, success. My beauty let me down and now it has abandoned me, just when I feel I need it most.

Yet sometimes I feel that my beauty never belonged to me, but to my parents instead. It was a gift that they bestowed on me, then, Indian givers, took back.

My parents were obsessed with the way things – houses, objects, clothes, everything – looked. And, when it came to people, their perception was distorting in the extreme. My father, narcissistic and, when young, as handsome as Adonis, set an abnormally high store by physical perfection. Claiming an aesthete's privilege, he used to say that he could not sit down to dinner (or presumably to any other meal) with an ugly woman. Such a woman, he said, was an affront to his artistic sensibilities; she outraged his sense of beauty, his notion of what was proper in the female sex.

One August, when I was seventeen, we went to stay

with a painter friend of his who had a house in the north of Greece. After lunch, I went to take a siesta. It was hot and I lay on the bed wearing only a pair of fuschia-pink bikini pants. As I drowsed, I heard the door open and then my father's voice. 'Look,' he said, 'isn't she perfect?' He had brought the painter to admire his beautiful, sleeping, almost naked daughter. I didn't move and then I heard the door close softly behind them. I've never forgotten that moment. It gave me such a strange, not altogether pleasant, feeling to hear my father talking about me in that way, as if I were an object, albeit a lovely one.

My father admitted openly that he had married my mother as much for her beauty as any other qualities. I don't know whether my mother had learnt her fastidiousness from my father, but she dieted relentlessly to please him, and her idea of a relaxing holiday was a week at a health farm. She once asked me, apparently seriously, if I thought my marriage would have lasted if I had been thinner (*she* would love me more if I were thinner, so she assumes the same would have been true of my husband – but lack of love was not the problem). Yet she claims never to have believed that she was beautiful; one of her oft-repeated stories from her childhood was of how her brothers had made fun of her legs, saying they were fat. This early trauma, she maintained, had left her with the unshakeable conviction that she was ugly.

Despite all this, I think that, in the year before he died, my father made various attempts to show me that he did love me. He was, I believe, aware that he had hurt me and wrote to me several times, but I was blind to the message in his letters.

When I told Louis what my mother had said, he put his arms around me and kissed me, kissed me to comfort me, as one would kiss a child, and said, 'I know you don't believe your father loved you, but he did.'

Six

One weekday Louis took a break from work and came, unexpected, to Oxfordshire to see me.

I had left London just over four years before, when life in the city had become too frightening (from a social, rather than a criminal, point of view – I wanted a break from worrying about party invitations) and too oppressive. It had also become too expensive for me. I was in the process of changing my life and no longer had – or wanted – a high-powered, well-paid job. I thought that if I lived alone in the country, I might be able to write. That was how I had spent my last four years – travelling and writing. I was successful in a small way and moderately happy. Work had taken the place of romance.

I went to live near Oxford because it wasn't too far from London and there were frequent trains. It so happened that there was a house available which I could easily rent and just about afford. I knew a few people in the area and thought accordingly that I wouldn't be lonely. I had vague visions of a social life involving dons, the university, dinners at High Table. As it turned out, I saw almost no one; my only local friends were a young couple in the village whose lives in no way overlapped with my own, though we got on very well. Our shared interests were our pets, the garden and I enjoyed cooking for them. It was true that friends from London some-times came to see me but the house was small and, in the winter, unappealing. Also people who live and work alone develop a rhythm into which it is hard to integrate other people. I found guests generally disruptive. I didn't know how to entertain them and I was glad when they left.

The house was a small, sixteenth-century cottage in a village with just one shop (which was also the post office), and a pub with the somewhat provocative name of The Black's Head. It was on the corner of a sur-prisingly busy road where there were quite frequently accidents, caused by drivers who rounded the blind curve at high speed. In addition to this disadvantage, the house was shabby and in dire need of redecoration. The ceilings were low, beamed and blackened by smoke and, on a grey day (God knows, Oxfordshire winters set a new standard in greyness), you needed to keep the lights on downstairs in order to be able to see anything at all. Central heating was non-existent and the hot water supply depended on a solid fuel stove which required, like a ravenous beast, to be fed – incessantly – with coal.

The maintenance of this stove was a precise science which, even after four years, I had not completely mastered. In consequence, it often died overnight and, when I woke up, the house would be freezing and I would have to address myself to the laborious, meticulous business of relighting it.

Sometimes, instead of merely going out, out of sheer perversity, it seemed, the stove would do the opposite and overheat. The water in the tank would start boiling furiously in the middle of the night and I would be awakened by knocking and banging. I'd have to get up and run the hot tap into the bath till the tank was empty; otherwise, apparently, it would explode.

It became a point of honour to master the stove, to get it going again, and at midnight, as I stumbled out to the bunker to fetch in the coal, in my slippers or even on bare feet, I felt a sense of achievement, as if I were a pioneer or a frontiersman.

Louis had taken an early train which got in around eleven. It was a bright, windy autumn morning and almost immediately we set out to walk across the fields on a footpath that led to a tiny church, used only in summer by candlelight, and the ruins of a Jacobean manor house which stood on the banks of a stream, a tributary of the River Cherwell which flowed all the way from Oxford. At some point in the seventeenth century a careless chambermaid had left a pan of hot oil on the fire in the manor-house kitchen and the entire place had gone up in flames, burnt nearly to the ground. I found these ruins intensely romantic – the spectacular jumble of broken stone overgrown with ivy and moss seemed faintly spooky, evocative of a dramatic past. A pastoral effect was confirmed by the grazing sheep. I often fantasized about somehow obtaining permission to rebuild part of the ruin, then living in it.

Louis was wearing an old jacket of my father's which I had given him. It was the one my father had always worn out walking, a sort of grey-brown tweed with leather patches on the elbows: it suited him perfectly. He looked handsome and strong and as if he hadn't a care in the world. We walked down to the ruins, along the stream and then on for miles, not meeting a soul, the sun warm and the wind rough against our faces; the muscles in my calves ached. Eventually, we arrived at a pub on the banks of the Cherwell where we drank real ale and ate bread and cheese. It was one of those perfect days, a day when you think nothing can go wrong, when the world seems completely on your side. As we walked, we talked. We planned our future, our idyllic future, and we tried, through polite, almost formal conversation, to get to know one another, as if we were strangers who had found themselves sitting next to one another at a dinner party. Despite our past history and the powerful sexual attraction that existed between us, in fact, Louis and I barely knew each other.

So – what did I know about Louis?

I knew his first and last names, but not if he had any other names. I knew how old he was, but not the date of his birthday. I knew his address in London and his telephone number, but not where he worked. I knew his girlfriend's first name, but not her family name. I knew his ex-wife's name. I knew his father's name, but not his mother's. I knew that his parents were divorced. I knew where he had gone to school and where he had gone to university. And I knew what he had studied and the kind of degree he'd received. I knew that he spoke a number of foreign languages, but only because he'd told me so, not because I'd ever heard him do so. I knew that he smoked and had a good appetite. I knew he wore glasses for reading. I knew he liked to change his shirt twice a day and I knew that he was almost obsessively clean.

I knew how he made love, with what degree of desperate hunger and energy. I knew how his skin felt and his hair, and the weight of his body on mine. I knew the taste of his mouth, the touch of his hands. I knew how he made me feel. I knew that this affair was my last chance.

There was something else I knew, but it was dangerous knowledge and I was suppressing it.

As for Louis, well, what did Louis know? I expect he knew pretty much all the same things about me that I knew about him and one other thing too. He knew that I had rejected him when he was young and vulnerable. And, were he to acknowledge it, he knew that was why he wanted me so much.

When people are in love – or think they are – they assume that they have everything in common. Their love brings them together, breaks down the barriers, eradicates their differences, their incompatibilities, smooths the way.

'We'll travel all over the world. I'll take you to Peru, I'll show you Machu Picchu. I'll take you to Madrid. We'll go next weekend. I love Spain. I'm a Spaniard at heart, a *conquistador*. We'll live for ever and we'll be very happy,' Louis promised.

'We'll go to Angkor, to Borobodur. We'll climb mountains. I've never seen the Pyramids,' I said.

'I'll take you. We'll go together.'

What is it about travel and love? As soon as people fall in love, they want to go travelling or at least to make travel plans. Whenever I fall in love, I want to go walking in the Himalayas. In reality, I hate walking and I'm very unfit, but love – or lust – turns me into a mountaineer. A would-be mountaineer.

I don't really remember what we talked about – we were bubbling over with words, ideas, schemes – but it felt good. It felt real, as if we were communicating, as if I were telling him – and he was telling me – what really mattered to each of us. It felt as if we were building a bridge between us so that, in addition to the sexual bond, there would be this other, mental link to prove that it wasn't just sex.

We got back to the house in the late afternoon. It was as I opened the garden gate that I asked 'What about Sara?' (Louis' inability, or reluctance, to finish with Sara was a bone of only mild contention – my question was more than anything else a gentle reminder that this problem would have to be solved.)

'Well, I'll have to handle that carefully. She's been very good to me, you know, and it's been a long time.'

'Yes, you must be kind to her. Let her down gently,' I said magnanimously. 'But don't leave her with any illusions. Be sure to make it clear to her that you love me, and that's why you're leaving.'

'I will. I do.'

Inside, Louis took off his jacket and muddy shoes, stretched himself full-length on the sofa in the sitting-room and asked for a whisky. I went into the kitchen, poured half an inch of Scotch into a tumbler, added two cubes of ice and filled the glass to the top with soda. I carried the glass back into the sitting-room and placed it on the low table next to the sofa. Bending over, I kissed Louis on the lips. He reached up to stroke my breasts through my sweater. 'I'll be back in a minute,' I said, 'I'm just going to the bathroom.'

I returned less than five minutes later and found a different person. The alcohol seemed to have entered

Louis' bloodstream as rapidly as if it had been injected intravenously. His eyes were glazed and as he stood up, he staggered, lost his balance and tripped over the table on which I had put his drink.

'Come on, darling, I want to go and have a look at the church before we leave for the station,' he said.

'You're drunk,' I said.

'No, I'm not. Do come on, darling. Don't be difficult.'

He pushed past me out of the house and began to weave up the narrow lane that led through the woods to the church. I followed him, trying to get him back to the house before anyone saw us. He flung his arms sloppily around me, saying, 'Oh, sw-e-e-t-ie,' drawling the syllables, 'don't be cross.'

I pushed him away and he staggered again and fell on to the path. 'Bitch,' he said from the ground. 'Bitch.' The word seemed to come out of nowhere.

'Fat bitch. No wonder your father couldn't stick you.'

The remark stung – like a slap would. It was meant to. When I accused Louis of being drunk, which he was, he wanted to hurt me back. It was easy enough to do.

Suddenly then, after our perfect day, came the bitter taste of reality. There was a history to all this, a history that I had chosen to forget or ignore. This was the dangerous knowledge that I had been suppressing.

Louis had a drink problem. He was, not to put too fine a point on it, an alcoholic. Not a heavy drinker, an alcoholic. I had suspected this for years; people would talk about messy ends to parties, scenes such as one prefers not to witness, and I remembered, from before, his incredible thirst. It had concerned me – to the extent that, before returning his first call, I rang a mutual friend and said, 'Louis telephoned. He wants me to have dinner with him. How's his drinking?'

'He's trying very hard. He's all right if he sticks to white wine.'

'That's all right then.'

If.

But, as I was to find out in the weeks and months that followed, Louis didn't stick to white wine, or he hardly ever did. On our first few dates I think that he must have been exercising great control, or perhaps I was simply so preoccupied that I didn't notice. Also everything seemed strange then. I wasn't normal. I didn't expect others to be. I saw the world through a distorting prism. So, even on this occasion, I didn't really register the full extent of the problem, and by the time my world had steadied and I was able to appreciate (that can't be the word) the extent of the problem, it was too late. I was hooked.

Louis drank as if the drink was going to run out. He drank like a man who had been in the desert for forty days. He drank with a great, consuming, desperate thirst. And he had no discernible desire to stop. The only time he didn't drink was at work and then I wasn't there to benefit from his sobriety. One night he said to me: 'I'm only interested in three things: beauty, which is where you come in; money and drink.'

Sober, Louis was handsome, intelligent, brilliant. When he had had just a glass or even two, he was amorous, tender and sweet. But drunk, Louis was raving, often vicious, weaving, staggering, incoherent – and then he passed out. His fine, patrician features would grow foolish and blur as if they were made of melting wax. His voice would change too, go up an octave, grow faint. Actually the whole of him would somehow become less defined as he got drunker – unless he was in the grip of an irrational fury, in which case he would rage against stupidity, ugliness and women – he was obsessed with the notion that women were 'taking over', that lesbianism was becoming widespread, that there would soon be no room for men. He could never see what fears and terrors these diatribes revealed. He combined – classically – arrogance and insecurity. I couldn't reassure him.

He once told me that he had never made love sober. I said, 'What about in the mornings?' He said that didn't count. But most of the time his drinking had no effect on his ability to perform sexually. If anything, it increased his desire and his energy, though sometimes I would find myself wondering if he really knew who he was making love to. He would lose himself in sex ('But, darling, that's the point,' he said) and in drink too (doubtless that was also the point).

A friend to whom I voiced my concerns about Louis' drinking sent me a postcard that he'd found in a joke shop in Soho. It depicted the 'effects of alcoholic content of the blood'. There were five stages, each illustrated with a little drawing of a man in a suit in various stages of intoxication. Louis could have posed for every one of them. Stage one: *Breath odour, Careless, Fluent*; Stage two: *Flushed, Clumsy, Boisterous*; Stage three: *Staggering, Incoordination, Confused*; Stage four: *Unintelligible, Helpless, Stuporous*; Stage five: *Unconscious, Paralyzed, Life endangered*. Stages one to four became commonplace for us. Stage five was, I feared, always just around the corner. I had never had to deal with a drunk at close quarters. I didn't like it.

My mother's father had, she said, been a drunk. I hadn't known that. All I knew was that I was his favourite grandchild and we adored each other until one night when I was about ten. I was sleeping in my grandmother's bed, all pink and scented with that sweet, powdery, old-lady fragrance, and I woke up to a stale smell of whisky and tobacco and a rough whiskery presence. And then my grandmother came in and said, 'What are you doing there?' And my grandfather got up and went back to his own room and his own bed. And after that, I didn't like him any more and I wouldn't sit on his knee or kiss him. Sometimes I would hear him retching and coughing in the bathroom in the morning and feel disgusted. But for years I forgot all about the time he got into my grandmother's bed with me, until I was eighteen and he had been dead for some time. Then it came back to me. By then, I knew what an erection felt like and I realized that my grandfather had had an erection in bed with me.

There was always drink at home – wine with meals, as in France or Italy – and, in the evenings, my father drank whisky-and-soda. When he got older, he drank neat vodka before lunch and whisky at night, but he always was a steady, rather than a heavy, drinker. He rarely got drunk – he had a good head which I have inherited – and then only when he was older and very bored. My mother didn't like his drinking at this point, but it didn't bother me. It was like my own: consistent, but rarely with obvious effects. My friends, mainly journalists and lawyers, had heads like rocks. They all drank, except for those who had over-indulged during the drug-fuelled years of the Seventies and early Eighties and had been dispatched to clinics, emerging some months later as teetotallers and pillars of Alcoholics or Narcotics Anonymous. We used to say, 'It's only people with a drink problem who have to wait until after twelve or after six. Those of us who have it under control can drink any time.'

I was once in Hong Kong working with a photographer and we had to get up at four to catch the dawn light. Around seven, we went to breakfast in a minute *dim sum* restaurant in the emerald wastes of the New Territories. There was a choice of Chinese tea or San Miguel beer. I asked for San Miguel, my favourite beer at the time on account of its advertising slogan: 'San Miguel: A Real Friend'. The photographer turned to me and said, 'You're becoming quite a promising little drinker.' After that, my friends and I always used to call a drink a 'promising one'. 'Isn't it time for a promising one?' we would say to each other.

With Louis it was *always* and *never* time for a promising one. He had the worst head I had ever seen. He actually drank less than most of my friends, but to far greater effect. Alcohol, even in small quantities, acted as a catalyst, transforming him, spurring him on to further excess. The difference between two and three glasses was terrifying. Suddenly, like a werewolf in a schlock-horror film, he would change. The transformation wasn't a slow thing. It only took a minute or two, just the time it took to drain a glass.

You may wonder why I didn't react, when Louis attacked me on the path to the church, by banishing him immediately. For good. I did, of course, register the cruelty. At the time, what he said hurt me far more than the fact that he was saying it. Louis did not yet have the power to hurt me. But the incident chilled me. It was a warning which boded ill for our wonderful future.

Seven

Louis had to go up north to see his mother so I didn't see him for a while after this, though we spoke on the telephone most evenings. He was sober, except for once and then he was sweet, his voice blurry and affectionate as he offered to pay my debts, to set me on my feet financially (an offer, as it turned out, he could not afford to make). He had had to go out of town. I didn't mind a bit. In some ways it was just as well: it gave us a breathing space, a respite from intensity. Also, I was getting ready to move back to London and busying myself with preparations. My life in the country had been an experiment, and, as it had turned out, a successful one. I had been happy there, in the little house, despite its drawbacks. At one point, I had contemplated trying to buy it, settling there permanently, but then I realized that my existence in the country – solitary, unengaged, marginal – wasn't 'real' life. Now it was time to face the city again.

The memory of my last meeting with Louis dimmed. I edited it so that I remembered only the good bits: making love in front of the fire; sleeping together, joined at the hip like Siamese twins; walking in the sun. The flash of drunken malevolence faded into insignificance and was, in effect, forgotten. As the days passed, it slipped a layer in my memory, overlaid by more recent events.

On the soft, pale skin of my inner forearm, hidden by the sleeve of my sweater, there was a small, livid bruise where Louis had bitten me – in passion. The bruise lingered like a memory and acted as a spur to other memories. I would look at it and imagine Louis stretching above me, balanced on his elbows, lowering his beautiful head to bite into the flesh, and a shiver would go through me. I was sleeping badly and woke at dawn every day, sometimes even before, when it was still dark (the doctor, to whom I went for sleeping pills, diagnosed depression). In the silvery light of early morning, I sought to banish thoughts of my father, to escape from the reality of his death by thinking about Louis. I was physically so in love with him that I was in a state of permanent arousal which the hours in bed at night only aggravated. Waking, I would turn on to my stomach and slip my hand between my legs to make myself come.

My fantasies were rarely about Louis, though he was their stimulus. Usually I imagined myself in a sex club in Amsterdam with a man I had only just met. We are watching a live sex show. Centre stage a tall, black man is fucking a very thin, etiolated, white girl. They are positioned in such a way that the audience can see his huge penis sliding in and out of her body. She shows no sign of excitement. In fact, she looks half-dead. Also on stage are two naked men, one on either side of the couple. They are masturbating furiously; this is the part which really excited me. My companion takes my hand and places it on his penis, which is erect. As I touch him, I hear his swift intake of breath, then a moan, almost of pain, which he quickly stifles (at this point in the fantasy,

I am so near coming that I have to pause and take my hand away). At the same time, he puts his hand under my skirt inside my pants. It is dark in the theatre; no one can see us. All around, people are doing much the same. I can hear sighs and heavy breathing. The two naked men look to be on the verge of climax. Their fists are moving so fast that their hands are just a blur. I am very excited but I know that I won't be able to come in the theatre. Abruptly my companion gets up. He takes my hand from his penis, pulls me to my feet and leads me to the exit. As we leave, the men on stage, including the black man, ejaculate. Outside in the street, the man I am with pushes me into an alley and fucks me standing up against the wall. We both come almost immediately. In reality, in my bed, my hand between my legs, at the moment of orgasm I say Louis' name.

I don't know what it was about this fantasy that excited me so. I don't know why I had this fantasy. I don't know where it came from with its blend of voyeurism and exhibitionism. I hadn't read it in a book or in a magazine. Nor had I ever been to a live sex show, in Amsterdam or anywhere else. I had only once seen a couple fucking but that was in someone's house, late at night and drunk. I hated it. I pressed myself against the wall on the far side of the bed, closing my eyes and putting my fingers in my ears so as not to hear them, wishing to God that I was somewhere else.

And this elaborate fantasy, simultaneously sordid and thrilling, was so completely at odds with my sexual life with Louis, which was – I don't quite know how to describe it; I think maybe 'unsophisticated' is the word –

at any rate, utterly straightforward. He favoured the missionary position, which, despite its drawbacks, I have always liked: it makes me feel safe, enclosed. Cover me.

But I had to educate him to caress my breasts (he said that he was a 'leg' man; oral sex repelled or terrified him), and I had to teach him that speed is not of the essence. It was not in his nature to slow down; his love-making was fuelled by the same voracious, selfish desire which characterized his drinking. I often thought that, if ever I stopped desiring Louis, desiring him so much that I wanted to lie down in the street in front of him and beg him to touch me, I might begin to find his love-making predictable, even monotonous.

But something strange was happening to me: there seemed to be three, quite disparate, but equally strong forces at work in me. The first – though I don't think the order matters – was the death of my father and my inability to sort out how I felt about it; the second was the emotional need which this had exacerbated and which I was trying to meet with Louis; the third was the all-consuming sexual hunger which he had unleashed, and which he was only partly able to satisfy.

I dreamed about Louis. I dreamed that we were driving up a very steep hill, so steep as to be almost vertical. The car started to fall, to lean out into the void. 'Quickly, lean forward,' I said. 'Lean right forward otherwise we're going to fall off.' When Louis next telephoned, I told him about the dream. 'Who', he asked, 'was driving?' I didn't know.

Louis returned to London. I took the train to Paddington to see him. He had been gone for ten days. I arrived late in the afternoon. It was cold now, there were no leaves on the trees; the interminable English winter had begun, we wouldn't be free of it till April. The city had a mournful feel to it. I felt mournful too, even apprehensive and tremulous, but also excited. Climbing the stairs, I noticed the stains on the pale blue carpet which covered them. The stains looked human, that is to say as if they were the product of the human body, rather than spilt coffee, or wine, or soup. Louis' apartment smelt the same as before. Sour.

Louis embraces me exuberantly and cracks open a bottle of champagne. Louis Roederer. I love champagne and take a conscious decision not to worry about its effect on him. All his glasses are chipped save for a couple of unbreakable French tumblers. Upstairs in the bedroom, before undressing, he pours the champagne and gulps down a glass. He is high, lit with the pleasure of my presence, burnished by the champagne. Immediately he is hard, immediately he wants to plunge into me. He doesn't seem to know about foreplay.

'Slowly, my love, slowly,' I say, 'there's no hurry. It isn't a race.'

But he can't slow down. He is desperate to make love to me, to fuck me, but not, it seems, to come. We fuck for hours – the champagne is long finished – until my entire body throbs and hums like a transformer, converting me from a lower to a higher voltage. Louis is priapic, hot metal. His excitement is exhausting but neither of us is able to come. We are simply too tense, too excited. Eventually, sheer fatigue compels us to stop.

Louis sits on the edge of the rumpled bed, smoking and talking nineteen to the dozen. Every two minutes he checks the champagne bottle to make sure that it really is empty, that there isn't a drop left. I know that he wants more drink but there is none in the house and he is enjoying himself far too much to get dressed and go out. He talks about everything under the sun: George II's mistresses; the relative merits of Wiltshire and Shropshire; his plans for buying a croft in Scotland; whether he will get the promotion he is hoping for; the impossibility of finding a 'good' yellow; the redecoration of his bathroom (which it certainly needs); the hopelessness of the present royal family; his loathing of all modern novels except for hard-boiled thrillers; the genius of Pushkin and Byron, his heroes, the latter particularly. Here he jumps up and, naked, rushes out on to the landing, returning with a volume of Byron's poetry. 'This is you,' he says, reading. 'She walks in beauty, like the night/ Of cloudless climes and starry skies;/ And all that's best of dark and bright/ Meet in her aspect and her eyes . . .' He is doing all the talking but I don't mind. He is immensely engaging and totally lovable. His erudition is dazzling. He knows it all.

I love the smooth curve of his neck, the way the nape fits into the palm of my hand, the pulse that flutters in his neck; I love his thick, brown hair – it's so thick that I have to force my fingers through it; I love his narrow, almost hairless chest – he has the body of an adolescent boy in most ways (he is, however, hung like a horse, a horse who can't get it down); his hairy, muscled legs are always a surprise; I love his skin, its silky texture, its blond smell. At this moment, he could be the worst drunk in the world and I wouldn't care. We are having such a good time. 'Tonight', he says, 'is when I really fell in love with you.' I know what he means. Sex is crucial but the acid test is when you want to *talk* to someone, to tell them things, all things, everything.

'You're mine,' he says. 'Mine, all mine.'

'Yes, I am. I belong to you.' I like saying that; it makes me feel secure. The way I feel right now I wouldn't object if he were to produce a branding iron and leave his mark on my ass.

But life moves on.

Louis' life was a delicate balancing act. He had only two modes: 'work' and 'play'; or, to put it another way, 'sober' and 'drunk' (or 'drinking' which became 'drunk' in the twinkling of an eye). If he wasn't drinking, he couldn't play. He couldn't go out, see people, even me, enjoy himself, make love, unless he had had a drink or two. He just couldn't relax enough. But if he was drinking, then soon he was drunk and then nobody wanted to see him or have him in their house. He was incapable of leading what most people would consider a regular life. The only way he could keep it all together was by exercising what was in fact (though it took me some time to realize this) phenomenal self-control.

Louis' inability to relax without drinking was one thing; the effect of alcohol on him was another. And as if that wasn't enough, there was more. One evening, we came back to his flat after dinner in a nearby restaurant. It was a Friday evening. Louis was to go the country with Sara the next morning (for some reason – work perhaps – his weekends with Sara were always very short, beginning on Saturday morning and ending on Sunday afternoon). I was watching the late news on television; Louis was packing a bag for the weekend. I could hear him crashing around in the kitchen, opening and shutting drawers and cupboards. Then he came back into the sitting-room and asked, 'Have you seen my pills?'

'No, what pills?'

'You know, my pills, the ones I have to take.' His voice held a slightly panicky note.

It was the first I had heard of any pills, the first I had heard of Louis having to take pills, except in his wild youth, when he had taken everything – pills, powder, whatever – but somehow I guessed that this was different.

'No, I didn't know. But never mind that. Where do you usually keep them?'

'In here.' I followed him into the kitchen and he pulled open a drawer. As far as I could see, it was full of pills.

'Aren't those the ones?' I asked.

'No, of course not. If they were, would I be looking for the others?'

I pulled the drawer right open and felt at the very back. Just more of the same wrong pills in blister packs.

'What do you need them for anyhow?' I asked.

'I'll tell you later. Let's just find them. Please. Help me.'

I knelt down on the floor and opened the cupboard below. It was full of china that appeared not to have been used for several decades. I started taking it out and putting it beside me on the floor.

'What are you doing?'

'Looking for your pills.'

What I thought might have happened had indeed happened. In his haste, Louis had pushed the relevant pack to the very back of the drawer, from where it had slipped down the back of the cabinet and into the cupboard below.

The pills that Louis was looking for, it turned out, were lithium. He was a manic depressive. He had been clinically diagnosed some seven years before, after a breakdown which had coincided with the collapse of his marriage.

Later that night, as we lay in a warm post-coital embrace, he told me about his illness, confiding the details to me like a precious gift. He told me that about seven years ago he had been walking up a hill and the world suddenly seemed extraordinarily bright and brilliant, sparkling like a great, big diamond; and he felt so great, as if he could *do* anything, as if he could just run up to the top of Everest or swim the Atlantic, as if he could *write* anything – the *Iliad*, *Ulysses*, *War and Peace*. Quite soon after, it had all come crashing down and he found himself in the bleakest, blackest despair possible. Now he had to take lithium, the miracle drug which slows down the over-active enzymes which result in mood swings.

But he didn't reveal that the effect of lithium is also to colour the world grey, to flatten the emotions, to make you feel physically heavy and lethargic, like a mere shadow of yourself. So manic depressives are often reluctant to take lithium even though they must, they absolutely must, otherwise they will go mad.

I didn't think any the less of Louis once I knew about his illness. But, then, I had no idea what manic depression meant (I took his brilliance for granted; it made him more attractive). If I had known more about it, I might have had a better idea of what I was getting into. If only, for instance, I had understood that manic depressives love the manic phase. If only he had thought then to tell me what he told me some months later: that one of the effects of manic depression is that the sufferer has no sense of the past or of the future. He or she is doomed (though at times this might seem like a blessing) to live forever in the present. Everything is *now*. Louis' seeming inability to comprehend that past bad behaviour had a bearing on the present, and his consequent conviction that I was sulking or bearing a grudge ('being horrid'), was a result of his illness.

But for my part, even once I knew this, I couldn't immediately just wipe out the memory (as he could) of his being hopelessly drunk and vile to me. I also didn't understand that, when he felt better, when he was in the upswing of the cycle, such as during one of those glittering evenings when time stood still, he would feel so good that he wouldn't take his pills because he didn't – in his view – need them. I soon learnt that, if he was drunk, he would forget (either deliberately or genuinely) to take his pills. When we were together, it was my task to remind him to take them. I understood now what he meant when he referred to Sara as his 'nurse'.

The pills lived in a drawer in his kitchen along with the Antabuse tablets. The Antabuse was to stop him drinking when all else had failed; it makes you so sick that you think you're going to die (some diehards have Antabuse implants: I heard of one who was so desperate to drink that he bit the implant out of his arm). In fact, I think, when you take it and drink, you nearly do die. Louis would swallow the Antabuse when he *had* to be sober; he was always terrified that I would muddle the pills and give him the Antabuse instead of the lithium.

It took me some time to understand that his reluctance to take his lithium paralleled his aversion to giving up drink. With the lithium, he felt dull. Without alcohol, he felt dull. Sanity and sobriety condemned Louis to a thick, felt blanket of greyness, a world without colour, without life or energy.

I don't know which came first, the alcoholism or the manic depression. I simply know that they fed on each other; like terrible twins, they egged each other on. I think (but I don't know) that alcohol diminished the effects of the lithium, made it less boring *and* less effective. For that reason alone, Louis shouldn't really have been drinking.

Why did he drink when he couldn't handle it? When he knew he couldn't handle it? The answer to that was clear: he drank because he was an alcoholic. His manic depression was separate, though it suited him to link the two. People say that alcoholism is genetic. Certainly drunkenness ran in Louis' family. His maternal grandfather, like mine, had been a drunk (albeit a more glamorous one). Louis was said to be the spitting image of this man who had died of a fever before he reached forty, after he had been wounded in the Spanish Civil War. At the time of his death, he had already been married twice. As a result, drunkenness didn't exactly have a bad press with Louis. It went with womanizing and love and war and danger and an early death before old age, infirmity and terminal boredom got you. Louis' *beau idéal* was Byron with whom he identified. It was no bad thing to be a tragic figure. And anything was better than being bored.

Louis also drank because he was unhappy and because

he was weak. Why, when he had looks, brains and charm in abundance, was he so unhappy? He had certainly had a difficult childhood: his parents had gone through a messy, bitter divorce. He claimed to hate his mother – he once told me, 'I wish I didn't have a mother.' It wasn't clear what the reasons for his antipathy were. She was 'cold', 'unsupportive'. He called her the 'Wicked Witch'. I wondered if perhaps she couldn't bear his drinking.

But other people have unhappy childhoods, cold and unsupportive mothers and violent, abusive fathers, and they don't feel the need to drink themselves into oblivion. It was almost as if Louis' gifts – his beauty, his talent for languages (he could speak six or seven), the glittering career that was his for the taking – were too much for him. He had to spoil it.

Louis claimed to love me more than life itself. Nevertheless, without meaning to, I contributed to his nervousness. As a consequence, it was virtually guaranteed that, in my company, he would drink *more* and take his pills *less*. Unwittingly, I set a standard to which Louis was always trying to measure up; the result, no doubt, of something that dated back to when we were first lovers. At its most basic level, it seemed that Louis didn't or couldn't believe that I loved him. I, for my part, didn't trust him (maybe I couldn't trust any man), perhaps because of the way that things had gone with Damon. I don't know if one ever really gets over an early betrayal. Certainly, we didn't seem to be able to. Yet it seems to me now that I had always known that love would bring pain, that built into the whole business is an atavistic awareness of inevitable suffering.

We were colluding in a *folie à deux*, which I, as the stronger partner, should have resisted. Circumstance and grief had made me weak. I can see now what Louis was trying to do: to lead a normal life, something which wasn't ever going to be possible. I didn't understand (how could I?) what he was going through. Had I understood it, I don't believe it would have made anything any better.

At the time, however, I took it all day by day. I never saw the big picture. It seemed sheer perversity on Louis' part not to take his pills and to drink himself into a stupor. Why couldn't he, I wondered irritably, just *pull himself together, get a grip*? And, if he really couldn't do that, why didn't he see a doctor, a better doctor? While I was exasperated by what seemed like hopelessness or wilful self-destruction, our attraction to each other was so overwhelming that I forgot about the difficulties as soon as I left him and longed only for the next occasion when we would be in bed together. All I wanted was to be with him in the little, white bedroom where our love-making took on an almost mystical quality. It was the only thing that made me feel alive, the only connection I had with feeling. He was, like the song says, 'in my blood like holy wine . . . so bitter and so sweet . . .'

High above the streets, in our pale chapel, under the eaves, like Balinese dancers whose every gesture is weighted and considered, we celebrate our own personal fertility rite. Nothing else matters. Still battered from the shock of my father's death, I have regressed and turned inward. Like the flies that come inside to die at the end of summer, when the weather turns cold, I am listless, dizzy, powerless to move. Caught up in myself, fragile, fragmented, I notice that the world has shrunk: Louis, the bedroom, the bed, the warmth beneath the duvet, his slender, dry, muscular body. Louis hovers above me as a humming-bird hovers in the air, treading invisible water, its wings beating to keep it aloft. He makes love silently; he never says a word, except once, as I begin to come, when he says, 'Open your eyes.' I open them and he moves inside me with not even a gasp. No little cries, no endearments, not even a moan nor sigh of pleasure break the silence.

Those weeks before I moved back to London were, in their strange way, almost perfect. I never thought to ask Louis why he didn't have to be at work, how it was possible for him to spend whole afternoons at a stretch in bed with me. It was the ultimate secret affair – there was no way that it could be integrated into everyday life.

That is what gave it its erotic charge, what made the sex so poignant.

Eight

Everything that happened between us, everything that Louis did with regard to me, every move he made, seemed deliberate and to have a purpose. Our shared past, which extended even beyond what I knew about, and was a part of, had for me, for us, enormous significance – as did the way we kept coming together. Louis too was the child of a diplomat who had been stationed in Peking; he too had gone skating on the Summer Palace lake; one summer, just before I got married, I had unwittingly taken the exact same cottage in Shropshire which he used to rent; sorting through old letters of my father's, I found a correspondence with Louis' father, dating back to the 1950s.

We could not ignore or dismiss the recurrence. It was more than coincidence. It had to be. Over the weeks that followed our initial reunion I had scrutinized my diaries for references to our past and found that I had documented every meeting. Louis *remembered* things about me, about us, that I had long forgotten and couldn't recollect even when reminded and that touched me hugely. The past was our country and our love was largely composed of that past. We actually had little in common and communicated badly, but need cries out to need and he had come back to me at a time when my need was great.

We placed far too much faith in this past. The fatality of this new encounter should have warned me that it was doomed. I thought that, because Louis had come back into my life just as my father was leaving it, it was meant to be. This time it was destiny, and therefore it would be fine. Even Louis' shrink, an eighty-seven-year-old Jungian in Chelsea, whom he was supposed to see once a week but often cancelled, thought that it was a good idea.

'N. thinks you're my future,' Louis told me more than once.

I believed him because I wanted to, though, in my experience, shrinks didn't say things like that.

It was, however, becoming apparent that we couldn't go on as we were. Sex and destiny were not going to be sufficient. Difficult people need difficult people – or so I've been told – but this was too much. I asked him whether he had discussed our difficulties (his drinking was the chief one, in comparison with which everything else seemed minor and manageable) with his shrink and, if so, what the shrink thought.

Louis repeated: 'He thinks you're my future.'

This time I said: 'And you think I'm your past.'

'*You* think I'm your nemesis,' he answered.

I repeated this exchange to Fleur, who was still my closest friend. She looked at me in astonishment and said: 'You don't actually talk to each other like that, do you?' But we did – almost all the time. We were forever having these sorts of conversations, as if they, instead of discussions about the evening's entertainment or about mutual friends, were the small change of everyday life. (This was perhaps because going out was fraught with difficulty and we had no friends in common.)

Fleur was the only person who seemed to realize why I put up with Louis. She understood the link between him and my father, between the past and the present, but that didn't mean she thought he was a good thing.

'Be careful,' she said. 'This is dangerous for you. You could get really hurt. Damaged people damage.'

During my years in the country, Fleur, who lived nearby, had several times invited me to local social occasions and had asked, as my date, a widower, a middle-aged country solicitor. His wife had died young and their only child was a diabetic. Now they both lived with his elderly mother.

'He's so nice,' Fleur insisted. 'Why don't you go out with him? He'd be kind to you, take care of you.'

'Oh, please,' I said, 'can you see me with his mother and his sick child?'

She laughed, 'No, not really.'

The solicitor was everything I didn't want. But so, really, was Louis. He, however, *looked* right and I had been raised to believe that looks mattered.

It wasn't long before everything began to fall apart. There was another, bigger crisis with Sara. One morning, after a night which we had seemed to stay awake throughout, Louis said, 'We can't go on like this. I'll always love you but we mustn't see each other any more. Perhaps we can be friends.'

Kissing him, I said, 'You know you'll never be happy without me. You can't be.'

But I found myself slipping away. Literally. Physically removing myself from the zone of engagement, the battlefield. Whenever the opportunity came to leave, I seized on it.

The first time I went for a few weeks to the Caribbean, a place that I knew and loved, where I had felt freer and happier than anywhere else. There I saw the man whom, for a couple of years, I had thought that I loved, whom I had actually loved, inasmuch as you can love someone who is thousands of miles away, married, and with whom you have not had, and are never going to have, a physical relationship.

'Are you in love?' he asked.

'Yes,' I said. 'You'll be glad to know that I have found unhappiness with another.'

In Antigua I justified my failure to telephone Louis by telling myself that it was too expensive, but the truth was that I wanted a rest. Louis, or rather my involvement with him from which I worried that I might be unable to break free, was beginning to frighten me.

After the Caribbean, I flew up to New York and very deliberately slept with two men. I wanted to put some distance between me and Louis, almost as if I could literally, physically interpose another body between us. But it didn't work. Oh, I enjoyed my romantic evening in the Village; I enjoyed it very much. My date, a man whom I liked and would one day learn to love, had filled his tiny, dark, one-room apartment with candles; reflections of their flames wavered in a series of mirrors and made it look twice as big. We lay stretched out on a mattress on the floor, ordered a Chinese take-out, watched old black-and-white movies, and made love. But the sex left me feeling empty and lost, as if it were not sex at all, but a pale imitation of the real thing.

Two days later, on my birthday, I ran into an old lover

I hadn't seen for several years. This man, older, powerful, full of charm and wit and intelligence, had had an enormous influence on me, an influence that had endured for a decade. His failure or reluctance to commit himself to me, to be the love of my life, still rankled, and I never could resist him. After my birthday party, we went to bed together, if making love standing in the deserted corridor of a New York apartment building can be called going to bed. But even that didn't do the trick: Louis' painful image was not to be displaced.

Part Two

[From our love]
I want neither
the sweetness of honey
nor the sting of the bees

Sappho

Nine

The great loves of my late teens, of my formative years, were Damon, naturally, and a boy called Ralph, who was the brother of a schoolfriend. While it may be fanciful to believe that these passions dictated the course of my later romantic career, it is certainly true that my willingness to suffer in the cause of what I believed to be true love (rather than a love within which I could be true, at least, to myself – since all my loves involved massive compromise on my part), combined with a kind of desperate promiscuity, can only have been the result of some profound lack in my early life.

In consequence, the fatal conjunction of sex and neglect did for me every time. It never occurred to me to turn my back on romantic love.

In fact, I had had a second chance with Damon, rather in the way that I was being given a second chance with Louis, or Louis was getting a second chance with me.

We had met again at my cousin Charlotte's twenty-first birthday party. I had a new, very short, haircut, a new dress that I didn't much like and a generally bad feeling about the evening. Damon was the first person I saw when I came into the room and – surprise, surprise – he was my cousin's boyfriend. I hadn't seen him for eighteen months. His hair had grown long, down to his shoulders, he had a beard and was shorter than I remembered him, but his eyes were the same, big and green and full of mischief. We went for a walk in the garden and, by way of making conversation, he said: 'You gave me crabs.'

I said: 'I couldn't have. I was a virgin.'

Then he told me that during the Christmas holidays, while I was pining and looking out for the postman, he had met someone else in Scotland. Her name was Marianne or Marina. So by the time we actually went to bed together, it was already over between us.

This meeting, just when I was beginning to feel better, reopened all the old wounds. (As Groucho Marx said: 'Time wounds all heals', or was it 'heels'? Either way.) Some months later, I encountered him again at Edinburgh University. It had been thought that I would go to Oxford or Cambridge and I had only put Edinburgh third on the list as a throwaway, romantic gesture because Damon was a student there. My parents were bitterly disappointed at my failure to be accepted by Oxbridge; their disappointment bordered on pique, as if they had somehow been cheated out of something which was their due. But this was nothing compared to my own feelings of shame (Fleur was going to Cambridge), which mingled with the bitter-sweet blend of anticipation and dread which I felt whenever I thought of Edinburgh, Damon and the future.

After leaving school, Fleur and I had been sent for the autumn term to a crammer in London, so as to get up to speed for the university entrance exams. I was lodged in a boarding-house full of girls all being similarly crammed. But once the exams were over, I moved in with a friend while I waited for the results.

Celia had been in my class at school. She was pretty with long, dark hair, freckles, a broken front tooth and a clumsy puppy-fat body, the second of eight children – three boys and five girls – whose father, a dentist, had run off with his hygienist.

I adored Celia's mother, Ruth, and couldn't understand her father's desertion. I had met the hygienist briefly and, by comparison to Ruth, she looked dreary. Ruth, even after eight children, seemed young and so much fun. She had red hair cut in a dashing bob, wore short skirts and drove a sports car, which she let me drive and which I had damaged so badly in a collision that it had to be scrapped. She was incredibly easy-going; we could do whatever we liked. She didn't stop us drinking or smoking dope or staying up late or playing loud music. I loved staying at Celia's, not least because I had conceived a sudden passion for Celia's older brother, Ralph.

Ralph was then a student at Oxford, a dark, androgynous beauty with perfect teeth, with theatrical ambitions and some talent, both as an actor and director; he was a leading light in the Oxford University Dramatic Society and had even appeared in films. Born on Midsummer's Day, he dressed like a medieval page in capes and jerkins of russet-brown or green, close-fitting, velvet trousers and soft leather thigh-high boots – a cross between Puck and Robin Hood. Rather than seeming eccentric in these clothes, he simply appeared beautiful. He was dreamy, self-absorbed and moody. When he smiled, showing those perfect white teeth, it was as if the sun had suddenly come out on a cloudy day. He was fatally attractive to men as well as to women; it wasn't at all clear which sex he preferred. I don't think he much cared. Probably he was simply a narcissist who enjoyed the adoration that he inspired.

Ralph never showed any interest in me, but it wasn't long before I was brooding over his every word. If he said, 'See you later' or 'Talk to you soon' or 'Don't go away', I would clutch the phrase hopefully to my heart, convinced that it had a secret meaning. I knew that he had a girlfriend in Oxford, a budding actress, but this knowledge did nothing to diminish my yearning for him. Then, one evening, we found ourselves alone in the family house. Ralph was back from Oxford and soon to go to New York to play the title role in *Tommy*, off-Broadway. It was just before Christmas and I was about to leave England to return to Greece.

In the basement of the house was a den with an open fireplace; it was furnished with big brown floor pillows and a record player and television. We all spent most of our time there. When Ralph was home, it was his domain.

That night we had been smoking dope. Without warning, he slowly leant across and began kissing me softly and stroking me, everything in marijuana-fuelled slow-motion. I couldn't see his face for hair, his dark hair tangled with my fair hair. As he touched me, he watched my face with a strange half-smile. This went on for hours, or maybe minutes. I lost all sense of time. When we were finally completely naked, lying on the cushions in front of the fire, he said, 'We can't make love, we haven't got a contraceptive.' I laughed and said, 'It's OK. I'm on the Pill.'

But we didn't make love; I don't know why. Ralph suddenly went silent and sad and huddled up into himself. When I asked him what was the matter, he said he didn't want to go to America, that he was confused and wanted to live in a forest and grow unconfused.

Eventually, he went off to sleep in his little room adjacent to the den and I climbed the stairs to my room. The next morning, he flew to America and I flew to Athens.

After the holidays were over, I returned to England by car with my father. One evening, on the way, when we had stopped for the night in a small town, just over the border into France, he asked me, over dinner, how many men (men? boys, perhaps) I had slept with. Emboldened by the wine and by his air of dispassionate interest, I told him. 'Five,' I said – no more than the truth.

My father wasn't *visibly* shocked. All he said was 'Why?' I told him that we believed (or believed we believed) in living with our bodies rather than with our minds and that sex was a wonderful means of communication. It was actually the best, the truest form of communication. He just said, 'Mmm' and nodded. He didn't ask me to go into detail.

Back in London, I settled down to wait out the year before going to university. Fleur and I set up home together on the top floor of my aunt's house in St John's Wood. My aunt made a self-contained flat there for two of my cousins who had now left home. It had a couple of big, light bedrooms – each with its own old-fashioned gas fire that popped and spluttered and gave off a blue light and a faintly poisonous heat – and a bathroom and kitchen. I loved the flat, I enjoyed having Fleur to myself and I loved playing at being grown-up.

My aunt was amazingly tolerant. Most evenings a group of us would sit on the floor, smoking dope and playing records – Bob Dylan; gloomy Leonard Cohen, the poet of our hearts; Syd Barrett; Jefferson Airplane; Fleetwood Mac; the Doors; Cream; the Velvet Underground. I remember a line from a song which seemed perfectly to capture the mood of that time – something about the days being bright and filled with pain. We were always smoking dope. I can't now remember what I felt about marijuana – whether I really liked it, I still can't decide if I do – but then it was *de rigueur*. We got stoned every day, regardless of what we had to do. Driving, working, crossing the road, buying a pint of milk, washing up, sleeping, dreaming, fucking, listening to music – we did everything stoned.

The boys liked electronic music best – Jimi Hendrix, Cream; they would mime frantic guitar-playing to it and shake their heads wildly. I preferred long, pretentious ballads full of apparent truths about love and loss; Bob Dylan or Leonard Cohen for choice – country music was way too sentimental, too immediately appealing.

For much of that year, despite yearning for Ralph, I had a boyfriend called John who I had met while he was going out with Celia. John had curly hair and round wire-framed glasses like John Lennon's. He had been on the verge of seducing Celia, then still a virgin, when I showed up and took him away from her. He was older than us, about twenty-four, and shared a flat near Tottenham Court Road with two women. Both women

were attracted to black men and would pick up different
ones most nights in clubs, then bring them back to the
flat. John had a tiny room with a mattress on the floor;
the women would return late after we had gone to bed,
and then the record-player would start up. John called it
the 'sex machine'. We never saw the men they brought
home.

Fleur was having an affair with a serious, dark-haired
boy called Sean who also smoked a lot of dope. They were
in love and thought that it would be for ever. Even so,
one morning after I had gone to work, she crawled into
my bed and had sex with John. She told Sean about it; of
course, he was furious. He told her that she'd 'violated
his innocence'. Another time, I went to bed with the tall,
skinny brother of one of John's flatmates. He was a
Jewish boy called Jacob, with a long, thin penis to match
his long, thin body. He was so bony that his hips left
bruises on my inner thighs.

I told John about it but, unlike Sean, he didn't mind.
Far from it, he and Jacob discussed me. 'We decided that
you take your affairs very seriously but at the same time
they're all just one big movie.' I didn't mind John sleeping
with Fleur either.

Another evening, John and Celia and I had a sort of
threesome, what Celia called a 'group grope' – nothing
very intimate, nothing penetrative, just kissing and
cuddling. I seem to remember that it was supposed to
make Celia feel better about my going off with John – she
had really liked him – but I don't expect it did. Ralph was
away at university and I hardly ever saw him except on
the occasional weekend when Celia and I went up to
Oxford. They did a lot of Shakespeare there; we saw him

in *Coriolanus*, *Hamlet* and *The Tempest* – all in the space of six months.

I found a job in the book department at Harrods. It was extremely badly paid and you got hell if you were discovered making, or even receiving, any personal telephone calls. I had been working there for a couple of months when I started to feel an itch in and around my vagina. The itching was terrible. I couldn't sleep at night. I scratched so much that I rubbed myself raw. When I told John, he said that I would have to go to the VD clinic. I made an appointment for it during my lunch-hour, but when I got there I didn't realize that you had to announce yourself. So I sat on a bench and waited for over two hours, until a nurse came to ask me what I was waiting for. Then I saw a doctor who immediately diagnosed thrush – nothing too shaming – but my lunch-hour was long over and I was already in trouble for making and receiving personal phone calls, which the manager of the book department claimed was the equivalent of stealing from the company. I left the clinic, not knowing what to do. I didn't dare go back to work. I met John in the street – he lived near the hospital – and he put his arms around me and said, 'Fuck the stupid job. Fuck Harrods.' About ten days later, an old uncle of mine called me at the book department, only to be told, 'She went out to the doctor and never came back.'

I got another job, through a connection of John's, working for a small environmental lobbying group, which had a basement office somewhere in the tangle of streets round Bloomsbury. I had to file newspaper cuttings, type a few letters and reports and run documents through the old-fashioned Gestetner copying machine. I liked it there. Fleur got a job with a man who owned a printing business – letterheads, menus, wedding invitations. She spent all her time intercepting calls from his wife.

One weekend in July, John and I went away to spend a few days in a cottage in Wales. A couple of lesbians lived there, friends of John's from way back; they had retreated to the countryside to pursue their love away from prying eyes. The tiny cottage had neither running water nor electricity. It seemed very romantic. John and I made love under a feather eiderdown with a rose-patterned cover. The girls were taciturn; Jo was tall and brown with a thin, brown face and brown hands; Penny was smaller and blonde with a compact, round, little body. During the day, John and I went for walks and wished that we too lived in a cottage without running water or electricity. One afternoon we climbed to the top of a round, green hill, not talking at all. The day was very hot and windy. At the summit, I was so hot that I took off my t-shirt. John cut an orange into quarters and squeezed the juice on to my bare breasts and licked it off. 'You're a lost cause,' he said. 'Given up to the pleasures of the flesh.' Walking down the other side of the hill we came across an empty house and fantasized to each other what it would be like to live in it. The door was secured by a flimsy lock and it was easy enough to break in. In the kitchen there was an old-fashioned, solid-fuel stove, its enamel chipped and rusty, and a big, old, porcelain sink, which you could almost have taken a bath in. The floor was littered with the droppings of small animals. Upstairs a damp, horse-hair mattress stood propped against a wall. John laid it on the floor and drew me down beside him. We made love in the late afternoon sun and afterwards whispered to each other about how our lives would be there.

'We'll have a cow – for milk,' he said.

'And sheep. I want sheep – for the way they look in the field,' I said.

There was no talk of babies.

Later John and the girls walked several miles to the village hall where an all-male choir was to give a concert. I couldn't face it and stayed alone in the house, reading by candle- and firelight. I read R. D. Laing's *Sanity, Madness and the Family* and grew more and more spooked. I didn't dare go to bed on my own in case a madman came bursting through the door.

That night I had a recurrent dream. It was a dream about a kite, a kite like a plane – you could sit in it. It was being driven, by two middle-aged queens, to a big house where Damon's cousins lived, the ones he had been staying with when I met him. Along the drive, the kite wouldn't – or couldn't – take off and fly. When we arrived at the house, they were all sitting at a long table, having lunch. I was put next to a cousin of Damon's, whom I knew in real life – or waking life, as the shrinks call it. He didn't know me but I said to him, 'You look just like Damon' and kissed him.

A couple of weeks later I bumped into Damon at my cousin's twenty-first birthday ball and everything changed. I couldn't bear John after that and anyhow he was going off to Nepal on an indefinite quest. We were leaving the flat; I was going to Edinburgh and Fleur to Cambridge.

Ten

Before arriving in Edinburgh, I had made all sorts of plans – the kind of plans that you make in the abstract. I was going to be a recluse; I was going to take up yoga and Modern Greek, and I definitely wouldn't sleep with the first man who asked me to sleep with him. I was going to live alone and go for long walks in Holyrood Park – a vast natural wilderness in the heart of the city, spread round the extinct volcano known as Arthur's Seat. I had read about it in a guidebook and envisaged myself tramping soulfully over the huge mound, reciting poetry under my breath. (I did, in fact, go for one walk there, but I was followed by a man who claimed to have been raped by a woman; that was the end of that.)

Initially, I found university terrifying. As well as the complication of my feelings for Damon, I felt totally lost. No one spoke to me for days. If I had had lodgings in a student hall of residence, it might have been easier, but I had left it too late for that, so ended up staying with an elderly woman friend of an aunt; this, of course, exacerbated my feelings of alienation and exclusion.

Other students looked different from me. They seemed younger, were noisier and, apparently, were happier. The girls were giggly, the boys gauche. I had thought that I was about to begin a new life in Edinburgh, but the old me wasn't giving up without a fight.

I saw Damon three times during my first couple of weeks at university. The first time, he sat next to me during an English lecture – theoretically, he was a year ahead of me but he was inordinately lazy and, having failed a few exams, had to attend some of my year's lectures; the second time was in the street; and the third was at a dinner given by my cousin, his lover, who was unaware that he and I had once been close.

Not long afterwards I reversed my green Mini into a battered van in the university car-park. When I went to the driver's home, to see about paying for the damage, he told me that he took lodgers and I agreed to rent a room from him.

My new room was big, but crammed with furniture. It contained a rickety double bed covered with a red, candlewick bedspread, a slot-machine gas fire, a shabby armchair, an enormous, non-functioning fridge which my landlord used as a store-cupboard, two spindly, low deal and Formica tables, a couple of cheap, upright chairs, a wardrobe, several large cardboard boxes and a bedside rug. A single, bare light-bulb dangled from the ceiling.

A couple of weeks after I had settled into my new quarters, I acquired a boyfriend. While Damon – the possibility of seeing him, talking to him, even the knowledge that he was in the same town – was my *raison d'être*, his proximity was also a form of torture. My intense awareness of him left me wide open. I had no idea what, if anything, I was supposed to do about the situation. I didn't know if there was anything that I could do. I was used to Damon having all the power: his name, I had found out, derived from the Greek, meaning 'to tame' or 'subdue' and was often used as a euphemism for 'kill'.

At the same time, I continued to function in a perfectly – or relatively perfectly – normal way, just as when I was seventeen, once I had got over the initial blow of Damon's desertion, I made other relationships, even fell in love – or thought I did – with other people, people like Ralph. Though acquisition of a boyfriend might seem like proof of a lack of seriousness, a lack of real love, actually, it was nothing of the kind. In Edinburgh, I functioned on two simple levels: the Damon level and then on the other level. I coped because I was able to draw on a mechanism which I had developed to deal with everyday life. My feelings for Damon and the damage he had done to me were, I decided, like a disease in my blood, or a birthmark in an inaccessible place – always with me but not visible to the outside world.

Stephen, my new boyfriend, lived in Glasgow, an hour's bus or train ride away. His brother was at Edinburgh University and, one Saturday, invited me and a girlfriend to a party. He said that we could stay over and sleep on the floor. That was how it began – on the floor, after the party. I don't think we made love that night, just cuddled. Stephen had shoulder-length blond hair, brown eyes and a smooth, compact body. His skin was soft and fair, like mine, and he smelt clean. Sex between us had an innocent, puppyish quality: it was unerotic and passionless, though comforting.

By now, the winter had set in and my room was freezing cold. Once the shilling's worth of gas ran out, unless you immediately put another shilling in the meter, the room quickly chilled. I woke up in the middle of the night and found myself frantically pedalling an imaginary bicycle in a pathetic attempt to get warm. In the morning, there were icicles on the inside of the big windows. When Stephen came over from Glasgow at weekends and kept me warm at night I was glad – and I was glad too, to have an excuse to leave Edinburgh.

But, in my eyes, Stephen couldn't begin to compete with Damon (of whose existence naturally he was unaware) and the relationship foundered amicably after a month or so. I went back to sleeping alone in my big, cold room.

At the time, it all seemed to take for ever, but I can see now that a train of events had been set in motion at my cousin's twenty-first birthday party which had all the inevitability of destiny. Whether or not Damon realized the full extent of the hold he had over me, he cannot have failed to sense something. I probably infected him with my urgency, with my longing, with my sense of unfinished business.

One afternoon in early December, shortly before the end of term, we ran into each other at a lecture. After it ended we walked out to the car-park. He had someone else's car – I can't remember why – and asked me if I would drive his own car back to his flat on the other side of town.

Damon shared a flat in the Georgian part of the city with Greg and Greg's girlfriend, a pale, slender, blonde student called Jenny. Greg was a few years older than us and had given up on university, half-way through his course. Instead he sold dope. They were both at home that afternoon and we all sat round the kitchen table, smoking joints and drinking whisky. This was how Damon spent most of his time. That was why he was having to repeat a year.

Marijuana and conversation don't mix at the best of times. The amount of breath needed to inhale, then the holding of that breath so that the drug can work its magic, makes talking difficult. Anyhow, who needs to communicate when you can just enjoy the vibes? We sat there for half an hour or so. As everyone grew more stoned and drunk, the conversation wound down until we were just sitting there in silence. There was no hurry. I knew exactly what was going to happen.

Damon took my hand and led me to a little bedroom behind the kitchen. As we embraced and lay down, he told me that, one morning a few days before, he had dreamt that he was making love to me; when he woke up, he found that he was fucking my cousin, Charlotte. After an hour or so, we got up and dressed. Damon picked up a necklace of milky glass beads strung on a silver chain from the bedside table and put it round my neck. Greg and Jenny had gone out.

I opened the window – the room had a gamey, jock-strappy smell. Outside the city was humming – not roaring as New York or London do – but humming as if many miles away a speedboat was disturbing a calm stretch of water. I thought of the old song, 'Speed bonny boat Over the sea to Skye': when I was little, I thought it was 'sky' because what was there on the horizon at the end of the sea but sky?

That evening, after supper, we went back to my room and made love with such energy and abandon that the old bed collapsed with a loud crash.

This turn of events, however predestined, however longed for, left me in a state of uneasy ecstasy, part terror, part rapture. I had been so shocked by what had happened between me and Damon the first time round that there was no way I could relax into this new state of affairs. The phrase 'the godspeed of trust' kept running through my head. The godspeed of trust was lamentably absent here. Trust, like virginity, once lost, cannot be restored; I had lost both simultaneously.

It was nearly the end of term. Christmas was drawing close. Damon neglected to tell Charlotte what was going on. Maybe he didn't know exactly what was happening, or he was waiting to see how it turned out or hoping perhaps that somebody else would do the job for him. But even a blind man would have noticed that she was worried. I was too but I needn't have been. One of his friends told me, 'Damon's so lazy that he'll come to you because you're there.' I didn't care about his motives, only his presence.

One evening I gave a dinner party in a flat which was lived in by some boys with whom I had become friendly. The true purpose of the dinner was to see Damon, who had not been around for a few days. I decided to cook a dish that I had often watched my mother make: chicken breasts sautéed with cream and marsala. I got the marsala – no mean feat in Edinburgh, where, in 1971, meat pie-and-chips or charred hamburgers were usually the gastronomic peak to which everyone aspired – and the cream, but I misjudged the timing, not realizing that the chicken was usually off the bone. When everybody sat down to eat, seduced by the wonderful smells, the pieces of chicken were still raw inside. I felt mortified.

Greg and Jenny stopped by after dinner. I opened the door to them and Jenny said, 'That's my necklace. Why are you wearing my necklace?'

'Damon gave it to me,' I said.

'Oh, really. Well, it's mine. Give it back.'

I took off the necklace and handed it to her.

After a lecture one morning, Damon and I were drinking coffee in the cafeteria in the basement of the ugly tower block where most of our classes took place. While we were sitting there, Charlotte came bustling in. She was a big girl and she moved with the sturdy force of a tractor. She saw us and strode across the room, her nervousness competing busily with her efficiency.

'Damon,' she said, 'I've been looking for you for twenty minutes.' She stood there, looking down at us. After what felt like a lifetime, I got up and left them to it.

Charlotte continued in ignorance of the true state of affairs for a while longer. Damon moved uptown from Stockbridge to a flat near the university. There was a wide stretch of meadows between his flat and the campus. I left the room with the fridge and went to stay there too but I had my own room so Charlotte still didn't know that Damon and I had become lovers. I'm not even certain that she knew I was living there, though surely someone must have told her. It's amazing how long people can remain in ignorance of what they don't want to know. Damon was playing games with both of us. I never knew when or if he would want me.

One morning he called me into his room and told me to get into bed with him. I was wearing nothing but a short, black slip. Charlotte walked in on us. She had brought Damon some breakfast.

Charlotte had been the guardian of Damon's affairs. A man as lazy and impractical as he was – as he chose to be – needed a nanny, a social secretary, *une femme d'affaires*. This had become her role. The eldest of six children, five of them girls, she was the daughter of a cousin of my mother's who had married a rich woman. She was brisk, practical and kind, with a mane of fair hair and a modest private income. She was a nice girl – she is a nice woman now, a middle-aged woman like me. I see her sometimes at parties or in the street: she lives near me in London. She married a short, dark man and they had five children – all boys. She works as a history teacher, has done so for twenty years at the same school, and keeps her thick, still-long hair in a plait. She doesn't seem to bear me any grudges; I don't know if she ever knew what Damon meant to me. Perhaps she did and perhaps that was why she doesn't appear to hold that long-ago period of humiliation and deception against me. Perhaps she knows that I couldn't help myself, that I had no choice.

The Christmas holidays that year were suffused with *déjà vu*; they echoed the tension of two years earlier when I had been worrying about Damon and the future. I wrote long letters to him; I had nightmares about him; I played Janis Joplin's 'Piece of My Heart' over and over again and I gazed endlessly at a photograph of Damon, sitting cross-legged and naked, a huge spliff in his hand, and daydreamed that we would grow old together. My parents, in whom I did not confide, wondered what was the matter and thought I should see a doctor.

Soon after Christmas I drove across England to Suffolk, to spend a couple of days with Celia. Ruth had met David, a rich stockbroker with four children from a previous marriage, and moved with him to the country, to a rambling manor house in East Anglia. The house in London had been sold.

I was feeling schizophrenic as usual. This state of mind had become almost chronic as soon as I went to boarding-school in England and had intensified when we lived in Greece. In the summer holidays I always had a wild time with my Greek friends, going night after night to plate-smashing establishments with handsome dark men who drove expensive English sports cars. These Greeks were uniformly clean-shaven young men with trim haircuts and neatly pressed trousers; they smelt of *Eau Sauvage* and of sun. Their fathers were shipowners and politicians who wished to curry favour with my father. We would go to one of the many night-clubs along the coast near Voula, dance cheek-to-cheek for hours – I could feel their interest through my flimsy dresses – and then drive home in the early hours at dangerously high speeds. During the day, they – or rather, their fathers – had boats with which to take me out water-skiing. It was a life of luxury and pleasure, completely at odds with that of my girlfriends from school who, during the holidays, consorted with shaggy, dope-smoking Incredible String Band lookalikes.

Now the division in my life was a different one. It was between the old world – school, London, Ralph – and the new – Edinburgh and Damon. I was in love with Damon and was, if not exactly happy to be with him, in a state of hysterical euphoria about the prospect of a relationship with him (though, it must be said, I had no idea what kind of relationship it would be). None of this, however, appeared to make any difference to my feelings for Ralph, who was home for the holidays. When I saw him, I found myself as defenceless as before.

I think he must have sensed some difference in me because the first evening, after dinner, he took me up to his room, along a dark corridor at the far end of the house. The room was painted deep purple, the walls and the ceiling, and the sheets on the bed were purple too. He put some Pink Floyd on the record player and rolled a joint. I hadn't seen him for ages. During the months in London when I was sleeping with John, I hadn't dared to ask Celia about him and the few times I had bumped into him at their house, for all the notice he took of me, the evening that we had spent exchanging kisses on the brown cushions might as well never have happened. It was typical that, now that I was no longer in a frenzy of desire and uncertainty, he should make a move.

'It might be awful,' he said, peeling off my sweater. It wasn't, but nor was it magic.

Ralph had the slim-hipped, smooth-skinned body of a boy. There were a few curly, dark hairs on his chest, no more than a dozen, and a thin, straight line of soft, black hair that ran from his navel down to his groin. He had almost no smell and barely sweated. There was nothing earthy about our love-making. It was like a dance to which I never knew the steps. Ralph felt impossibly light, half my size and weight. By comparison, I felt heavy, clumsy, burdensome in his arms. I felt that he was honouring me with his embrace – his behaviour encouraged such sentiments.

On 31st December we drove to London and at midnight found ourselves in Trafalgar Square, celebrating the New Year amongst the crowds and the drivers blowing their horns and people jumping into the fountains and breaking open bottles of champagne. Ralph flung his arms around me and pulled me close to him.

Eleven

Damon was one of those men who had to have a woman. He would prefer some women to others – for instance, he liked me better than Charlotte, though I didn't look after him nearly as well as she did – but on the whole he wasn't terribly particular as long as there was someone.

In the early spring of 1972 there were power-cuts all the time, due to some industrial dispute. This suited us fine. We spent hours, sometimes whole days, in bed, unable to get enough of each other. The only other thing that Damon did, apart from make love, was smoke dope – incessantly. He couldn't get enough of that either, and scoring, or arranging to score, took up a lot of his time.

We almost never went out to see a movie, or a play, or even to visit friends. Our world was our room, our bed. We would lie there, making love, smoking dope and listening to records. André Previn's first wife, Dory, had just released an album called *Mythical Kings and Iguanas*; we played the title track again and again. Her high, sweet, fluting voice filled the room, floating up to the ceiling like a prayer to heaven. I'm not sure what we thought she—or we—was praying for, but her voice combined with the sex and the dope to create a strange, otherworldly atmosphere. It wasn't as if we were really in this world.

I took to regular sex as a drunk takes to the bottle. If

sex meant love, it also meant oblivion, and Damon kept me, like a sex-slave, fucked stupid, sedated. It was only when we were making love that I felt even vaguely secure with him; I wanted constant reassurance. I don't know if all women are like me: I have no sexual memory, or rather, none that lasts longer than twenty-four hours, and this was twenty-five years ago. So I can't really remember if the sex was good. If you are in love or think you are, there's no clear difference between good and bad sex.

Louis and I once had a discussion about the nature of good sex – for women. He said that it meant frequent, regular orgasms. I said, 'No, it's being in a state of constant, agitated, frenzied desire – when you just can't get enough of the other person.' The erotic charge lies in the desire, not in its gratification.

I wonder now whether I really believed this, or whether it was simply a theory that I formulated to justify, to tolerate the difficulties which I had with orgasms. It wasn't that I couldn't or didn't come – sometimes to do so was almost laughably easy, but it was never something I could rely on. Nor was it that I was frigid, or that all my lovers were inept – though, of course, some were; often I came with *those* ones as easily as rolling over. When things didn't work out, it was at least in part to do with nervousness – and inevitably trust or rather mistrust – a mistrust that got worse, not better as I grew older. I am pretty certain that I learnt to come with Damon; it also became clear enough over time that, in his way, he loved me. He had, however, an Englishman's reluctance to say so.

During the Easter holidays, we spent a week in my parents' house in Italy, the one where I had first slept with Louis. We drove, in my green Mini Countryman, for two days and a night across France, over the Alps and down into the Venetian plain.

I had very much wanted to go away somewhere with Damon. Despite the public nature of our affair, he still eluded me, kept me separate from him and in my place. He wouldn't take me home to the west coast of Scotland to meet his family. I didn't much care if he met mine – I wasn't sure what the point would be – but I wanted the recognition implicit in meeting his mother (his father had died some time ago). I wanted him to introduce me as his girlfriend. I wanted to be *official*.

Veering, as I did, between rapture and paranoia was terribly exhausting. Subconsciously, I suppose I thought that perhaps if he were to come to my house, as it were, into my life, there would be greater equality between us. The current imbalance was driving me crazy, sometimes, or so it seemed, almost literally.

The house which my parents had built clung to the side of one of those round Italian hills with a view that stretched for miles. They had chosen this part of Italy because a friend of my father's, an elderly woman writer, had been born and brought up there.

Viva's parents had owned a fifteenth-century villa in an exquisite, jewel-like, walled town where Robert and Elizabeth Browning had once lived. When her parents died, she had inherited the villa in which she lived for many years. But as the town expanded, the traffic noise, and the scores of boys tearing by on their scooters, became too much for her, so she presented the villa to the *comune* for a museum and built herself a massive house on a nearby mountain. She was anxious to have congenial neighbours and persuaded my parents to buy the land on the hillside below.

As a small child, I used to stay at the old villa. It was a fabulous, almost fabled, place. All the bathrooms were marble but ravishing. There was nothing vulgar or *nouveau* about them. There was also a wonderful garden, a secret garden full of narrow paths, bordered with high hedges, and hidden statues which seemed to appear suddenly out of nowhere. I found one statue particularly frightening; I think it must have been of Pan. It had a crooked smile and I hated to find myself suddenly alone with it amongst the cypress trees at the bottom of the garden.

Viva's new house was oddly graceless. It sat on top of its mountain like a great protuberance, dominating the lower hills, including the one where our house stood, and the valley below. But inside it was filled with treasures, objects collected during her wanderings throughout Asia Minor and the Arab world. She had recreated the marble bathrooms, with their shell-shaped basins, and the vast drawing-room, the size of a tennis court, had a huge picture window. There were often dramatic storms in this part of the country; from the big window, you could see the black thunderclouds bowling across the Venetian plain and the lightning forking the sky.

Viva was a brilliant woman but no beauty. Her mother had founded a small silk factory in the town where they had lived; this produced a thick, heavy fabric, not unlike Thai silk, and provided employment for a number of local women. When Viva was seventeen, her long hair had become entangled in one of the looms and half her scalp had been torn off. She lost her right ear in the accident. As a result, she wore her hair wound round her head, rather like a turban, to conceal the fact that she was missing an ear. She was short, barely five foot, and dumpy, with thick legs which culminated in tiny feet, of which she was extremely proud. She had fantastic, exquisite shoes made especially for her in soft leather and brilliant colours with ribbons and buckles and curved heels designed to draw attention to her perfect, delicate feet.

Viva's parents had arranged for her to marry a local businessman, but she had objected and, after the accident, no one insisted. Instead her younger sister married him and died a few years later, worn out by over-frequent childbirth and an unhappy marriage. Viva travelled and wrote books. In her forties, she married a fellow-writer. The marriage didn't last long. Her husband was a well-known homosexual who, I imagine, had envisaged some kind of *mariage blanc*, a meeting of true minds. Viva, or so the story goes, had been unaware of his homosexuality and bought herself an elaborate trousseau. The wedding night was a predictable fiasco. When, on their honeymoon, she fell off the back of the motorbike on which they were touring Turkey and, it was said, he failed to notice, it became clear to her that the marriage had no future.

Viva had met my father in Portugal during the war. She had fallen in love with him then and there and remained so all her life. She had wanted to marry him, but she was nearly twenty years older than he was and, as he absolutely had to marry beauty, he married my beautiful mother. He remained, however, very fond of Viva; he loved her mind, her conversation, her erudition – she had read everything worth reading, spoke fluently ten or more languages, including Turkish, Arabic and Farsi as well as the more usual French, Italian and German, and could read Latin and Ancient Greek with the same ease as if it were English. She didn't like my mother. She resented her and didn't trouble to hide her feelings. When we went to dinner at the big house on top of the hill, Viva would seat my father on her right and any other male guest on her left. My mother and I were relegated to the bottom of the table as far away as possible; she barely addressed a word to us. Viva thought that my mother was stupid and generally did what she could to make life difficult for her. One summer, however, when I was about fourteen, they found themselves unlikely allies.

A French woman friend of my father's came to stay for a few weeks. Our house was still under construction and my parents had rented a little house near Viva's, along the valley.

Veronique had married into the aristocracy. She had had two children by her husband, a French prince, and, though the marriage had long since succumbed to incompatibility and divorce, she retained the *hauteur* of her erstwhile marital status. She wore only couture, almost exclusively Balenciaga, who was then at the height of his powers – and, though not conventionally beautiful, she wore her long, chestnut hair in a perfect chignon and she was *très soignée*. She was also very rude and grand in the way that only Parisians can be, and she adored my father.

Veronique and Viva were actually very alike in many ways which is perhaps one reason why they detested one other on sight. Viva was torn between her resentment of my mother and her loathing of Veronique. The latter won out and for the rest of the holidays she and my mother observed an uneasy truce. I didn't like Veronique much either – she was even more unkind to my mother than Viva was. It was true that she had been nice enough to me when I was ten and had been sent to France for three months to learn her language. I had spent a month in her apartment near the Champs-Elysées, under the care of her daughter's governess, who would take me to the nearby Eiffel Tower or to the Tuileries gardens and correct my grammar and accent. In the early evenings, I had been permitted to go into Veronique's bedroom and watch her putting the finishing touches to her *toilette* before she went out. Her clothes were gorgeous. One evening, I remember she had been going to a masked ball. She wore a huge, pale-blue crinoline embroidered with stars and a matching, hooded domino and black velvet mask, all made for her by the great Balenciaga. She looked and smelt divine, like a wonderful, expensive fairy.

But, four years later, by the time she came to Italy, I could only see her as my mother's rival – her enemy even. One day, Veronique, my parents and I were having lunch in a restaurant. Veronique and my father were talking and my mother ventured to make a remark. Veronique, irritated by the interruption, turned on her. 'That is completely ridiculous,' she said. 'You do not know what you are talking about. You know *no*thing about it. *No*thing at all,' and she shrugged in that peculiarly

French way and looked at my father. *En toute complicité.*
My father said nothing. He certainly did not leap to my
mother's defence. My mother's eyes filled with tears and
she stood up, backed away from the table, then walked
towards the door marked *gabinetto*. I said to Veronique,
'I hate you. You're horrible. Why don't you go away?' and
ran after my mother.

Later, my father said to me, 'It's just Mummy's time of
the month.'

'But Veronique was horrible to Mummy.'

'Don't worry, I know Mummy. She didn't really mind.
I know more about women than you do.'

I didn't doubt this.

Soon after my father died, I started to make a list of the
people who had to be told. My mother said, 'Somebody
must tell Veronique, somebody must telephone her.' I
looked up her number in my father's address book. It was
an old, leather-bound book, whose binding was falling
apart; many of its pages were stained and full of
crossings-out, with scrawled new names and addresses. I
found Veronique where she had always been, at the
beginning of the 'R's. She still lived at the same address
in Paris where I had stayed. She hadn't moved in over
thirty years, but, when I called, there was no answer.
Eventually, after days of trying, not continuously, but
whenever I remembered – part of me was strangely
reluctant to speak to her – I found her at home early one
morning. She was just leaving Paris for her house in
Provence; the funeral was in two days' time.

Her response to the news of my father's death was
characteristic. She was furious that I had failed to reach
her sooner, claiming she had hardly been out of the

apartment for days; now she would have to change her plans, it would be difficult to get a flight from Provence to England, how would she get from the airport to the church, and so on. But her shock was manifest. Even over the telephone, she sounded as if I had punched her in the solar plexus and knocked the breath from her body.

On the morning of the funeral, my brother and I went for a long walk over the downs. I had a hangover which buzzed like a dentist's drill in my head from drinking nearly an entire bottle of whisky the night before. As we walked, we talked about our father and Veronique. I said, 'She was so upset when I told her. Surely they must have been lovers.'

'I don't think so. I think our father preferred to bind people to him by *not* giving them what they wanted.'

My brother was probably right. Anyway, I doubted that we would ever know the truth. Veronique took a cab all the way from the airport to the church. It must have cost her a fortune. And she brought a photograph for me, a photograph of me, aged about six, sitting on my father's knee, in some hot country. I still keep it by my bed.

Viva didn't come to the funeral. It wouldn't have been possible as she had died some years before. Died at a ripe old age, having suffered for some time from senile dementia. In rare lucid moments, she would remember my father and write him letters proposing expeditions on horseback to the foothills of the Himalayas or camel treks across the Empty Quarter. When he went to see her – which he faithfully did – she would sometimes recognize him and talk to him with all her old vigour, but, in these conversations, they were both young again. Before she lost her mind, this woman who had dominated so much of my early life, mellowed. She became friendly to my mother and friendly to me. When I went to visit her, I found her lying in a hammock on her terrace – she had sold the big house and moved into an apartment in the town where she had lived as a child. She was reading Homer – in Greek, of course. She said, 'I want to reread all of Homer, Virgil and Omar Khayyam before I die.'

Damon and I arrived at the Italian house in the early evening. The hills were velvety in the soft light of dusk and pigeons – those that had escaped the *caccia*-mad Italians – were cooing in the trees. I walked up the hill to say 'hello' to Rosa, Viva's housekeeper, and to borrow some milk. Viva was away in southern Spain, looking at the Moorish churches.

My parents must have had more money when they built this house than when they came to build its successor, the house in England. When all its additions had been constructed, that was ultimately bigger, but initially this house was and it was always more homogenous. A travertine terrace, with an octagonal fountain made of rough pink marble in one corner, ran along the front of the house, which overlooked the valley, and French windows led into the spacious room that served as both drawing- and dining-room. There was a bedroom for each child and two bathrooms.

My bedroom was upstairs at the back of the house. It contained a beautiful bed – what is known as an 'occasional double' – and not much else. My father had found the bedhead, which was French eighteenth-century and made of rosewood carved with round, hanging fruits, pomegranates perhaps, in an antique shop and got a local carpenter to make matching side-pieces and a footboard. When Veronique saw it for the first time, she said to me, 'I can just imagine you writhing in the arms of your lover in that bed'.

This longed-for sojourn in Italy remains strangely indistinct, like an image projected on to a screen which refuses to become sharp, however much you try to adjust the focus. Perhaps the fact that Damon had brought with him a supply of slender joints rolled with a cigarette-rolling machine, hidden in a packet of Benson & Hedges which he had carefully resealed, had something to do with this. We made daily expeditions to the small mountain towns, looked at churches and villas, ate pasta, drank lots of red wine, made love, slept late, but none of it is vivid. None of it mattered.

Somehow the holiday didn't do what it was supposed to do. It didn't achieve its purpose – which was to bring us closer together, to create a joint vision of the future. It was also the last time I ever went to the Italian house. My parents sold it soon after. When we arrived back in England, having driven through the night, Damon returned immediately to Scotland.

Twelve

Just as it was inevitable that Damon and I should get back together, so it was, I suppose, inevitable that we wouldn't live happily ever after. If the holiday in Italy had been a magical success or indeed an absolute disaster, no doubt I would be able to remember every detail of it. I suspect that the incompatibilities between us were beginning already to corrode the sexual passion and romantic desperation (mine) that had fuelled the early months. Fleur, who had contracted hepatitis at the beginning of her second term at Cambridge and so was forced to spend two months in an isolation ward, sent me a postcard; on it she had written, 'We don't want their love, we want their commitment.' I wanted both; to me they were one and the same.

All through the summer term that followed, I was hysterical. I suffered from constant mood swings and seemed to be in an unremitting frenzy of pre-menstrual tension, from which I could only be soothed by the act of making love. The act had a dual function: to reassure me that Damon loved me and to convince myself that I loved him. The initial sedative powers of sex had worn off and the intervals of calm grew shorter and shorter. Whenever I did get my period, the pain was excruciating so it is possible that my state of mind had some physical cause.

Damon, who was permanently stoned, suggested that I go to the doctor and ask for some tranquillizers.

The problem was that Damon and I actually had very little in common and, as the months went by, this became more and more apparent. He was the youngest of three brothers and, as far as I could tell, devoid of any conventional ambition. He came from a huge family and had a small private income which gave him security, even complacency, that was both enviable and infuriating. He had no desire to work, to make a name for himself, to *succeed* in the world. All he wanted was to buy a boat and sail it round the coast of Scotland. Other than that, he appeared to care only about smoking dope. Perhaps 'care' isn't the right word. He was, I suspect, addicted. He was very easy-going and at the same time phenomenally stubborn. If I wanted him, I had to fit in with him. 'Take me and leave me as I am' he would say when I stamped my foot in fury, but, for all that, he was extraordinarily tolerant of my hysterics. He had a passion for Hermann Hesse and would read over and over again *Siddhartha*, Hesse's story about a young Indian who meets Buddha and searches for the meaning of life. He gave me a copy for my birthday in my first term at Edinburgh, just after we began sleeping together again. I liked it well enough but it didn't change my life.

At the beginning of the summer holidays I saw Ralph again. Celia had called to ask if I wanted to go and see him in *A Midsummer Night's Dream*.

'It's the last night and there'll be a party afterwards,' she told me.

Ralph was playing Oberon. His beauty was undiminished and as I watched him stride about the stage in leggings and a short, swaggery cloak, I felt myself falling in love with him all over again. Edinburgh receded. A slender brown-haired girl with a fey expression, his girlfriend – or erstwhile girlfriend – was Titania. Celia said she thought that they had split up.

It was a warm evening and the performance took place outside in a college garden; it was such an English scene – the soft gold-coloured stone of the buildings, the tidy lawn, the roses spilling their petals and their scent into the night air. At the party afterwards, Ralph kissed me behind a rose bush and confusion set in.

Damon and I had made plans to go to Greece but that would not be for another month or so. I needed to make money to pay for the trip, so I got a job working in a charity shop in Oxford selling second-hand clothes and Third World artefacts. I worked an eight-hour day, from nine to five, fantasized about Ralph and worried about Damon. I sensed that Damon and I weren't going to survive as a couple for much longer and this knowledge tormented me – though not enough to try and make it better. I also worried about money. Somehow I had managed to forget to pay a whole month's rent on the flat in Edinburgh. What with my overdraft and the unpaid rent and Ralph's failure to telephone, despite having written down my number for the eighteenth time, and a great, cosmic anxiety about Damon and the future, the holidays were proving pretty bleak.

Damon and I did go to Greece in August. We arrived at Athens airport at three in the morning and caught an early ferry from Piraeus to the Cyclades. In Syros, the port looked so grim that we decided not to go ashore. Syros is the administrative capital of the Cyclades and full of wonderful, neo-classical buildings. But we didn't know this – or care. Advised by the ship's captain, we continued our voyage, finally disembarking on the little-known East Aegean island of Ikaria at four in the morning. We spent what was left of the night on a stony beach. Sleep was more or less impossible and when dawn broke, we tramped into town to look for a room. It took all morning to find one and, when we eventually did, it was cramped and smelly.

I hadn't been back to Greece for two years and the memory of my last summer there had persisted like a vision of Eden, a perfect idyll. I thought that, if I took Damon to the Aegean, everything would be OK again. But it wasn't. Nothing seemed the same. It was as if the Greece I had known and loved was another country.

This new Greece was uncomfortable and far too hot; I got sunstroke and spent twenty-four hours throwing up and feeling dizzy. There were hippies camping on every beach and crowds of tourists wherever we went. Damon couldn't see the point of it, couldn't understand what all the fuss was about. 'Why did we come here?' he would say. He missed Scotland and the North Sea, and his boat. Someone once said that Greece was like Scotland but golden instead of silver; somehow that summer it didn't look beautiful at all. We quarrelled every day and fucked with hate in our hearts.

The problem wasn't Greece, of course. It was that I was again obsessed with Ralph and spent long hours sitting in silence thinking about him. The phrase 'the summer that saw the end of my affair with Damon' went round and round in my head. But I always held back from breaking up with him, from saying the unsayable, from provoking the big quarrel that would mean the end. And so, when things became very bad, when we were barely talking and there was a horrible, tense, strained atmosphere between us, I would go over and put my arms around him and kiss him and tell him that I loved him. And we would continue together for another day. We left Greece and travelled to Istanbul. Damon paid for the trip. Nothing was any better there.

As soon as we got back to England, Damon took the night train to Scotland and I went to London and began to be unfaithful to him. I went to a party, took three Mandrax and soon found myself in bed with someone called James. The bed had a sky-blue velvet headboard. When I woke up in the morning, I had no idea where I was and had to ask James his name. I didn't have a clue what I wanted or what I was going to do. Every five minutes, I reached a different decision. These decisions were arrived at as randomly as if I had been guided by pulling petals off a daisy – instead of 'he loves me, he loves me not', I would say, 'I will break up with Damon; I will *not* break up with Damon; I will telephone James; I will *not* write to Ralph (who had finished at Oxford and gone to Lancashire to serve his apprenticeship in a provincial repertory company); I will *not* tell Damon that I have been unfaithful to him.'

Fleur had recovered from hepatitis and then spent the summer backpacking with Sean in southern Spain. Now she was at home in London, waiting to return to Cambridge. Her affair with Sean was running into problems too. 'Summer love ends when the summer ends,' she said. We had both hoped that our first love would be our last but this didn't look likely. In the end, I went home and telephoned Damon and told him that I had slept with James. He merely said, 'I guessed something of the kind.'

I drove up to Edinburgh for ten days before term began to resit an exam that I had failed in the summer. Damon had an exam to resit too and he was living with me. Now he said, 'I want it to work between us.' I said the same and for a week or so, it was almost like old times. I passed the exam and went back down to England. There I slept with the much older boyfriend of a schoolfriend and afterwards felt sick. I rang Damon and asked him where he was going to live next term. 'Away from you,' he said.

I don't know what happened, how the city, which had once seemed so small, suddenly became so huge so that we never once ran into each other again. As far as I knew, Damon did not have another girlfriend the whole time he was in Edinburgh. When he had finished university, he went back home to the west coast, got the maid pregnant and married her. They had a daughter. Now, I hear, he just lies in bed all day long smoking dope. People who have been to visit him, say that he has rigged up an elaborate system of ropes and pulleys in his room so that he can do everything from his bed: open doors and cupboards, turn on and off lights, summon his wife.

Often, when I have thought about Damon and what happened or rather has not happened to him, I have found myself remembering Somerset Maugham's short story 'The Luncheon' about a young writer who receives a fan letter from an elderly female admirer. He is enormously flattered and suggests a meeting. They meet for lunch at a restaurant of her choice and she orders all the most expensive dishes – asparagus, salmon, out-of-season wild strawberries. He spends the entire lunch worrying about the bill and, sure enough, when it comes, he can only just pay it. He is left with nothing to live on for the rest of the month. The story ends with the words 'But I have had my revenge. Today she weighs twenty stone.'

Now I am not so sure that I have had my revenge. I wrote in my diary soon after the break-up, 'A future without Damon and a past so full of him, it makes me sick.' Years later he came to see me in London. 'I always thought we would get married', he said, 'and live happily ever after.'

Thirteen

Soon after Damon and I broke up, I had all my hair cut off. I had it sheared to about half-an-inch all over; then I went and bought a bottle of silver shoe dye and dyed my platform boots and bought a pair of silver braces for my dungarees – the David Bowie/Ziggy Stardust look.

I also embarked on a spree of promiscuity which made all my previous efforts look tame. Within a matter of weeks, I had slept with Ed, Derek, Hilton, Andy, George, Roy, Derek and Martyn – the last two were a pair of actors whom I met late one night at the Traverse theatre; I ended up in bed with them both at their hotel. Martyn was slim and dark and reminded me of Ralph but I didn't like Derek much and of course he couldn't wait for his turn.

I spent quite a bit of time with the other Derek. He was a philosophy student, eccentric and clever; he wore all black clothes, including black leather gloves and sometimes an eye-patch – for show – and he had a thin, black moustache like Rhett Butler's. He liked to play me tapes of himself talking, holding forth on a variety of topics: determinism, formalism, existentialism, Marxism. That was his idea of foreplay. Actually, it was often his idea of sex.

Many years later this Derek heard me speaking on the

radio and wrote to me, care of the BBC. He invited me to lunch in Cambridge where he was living and where I was working part of the time. It was bleak midwinter, an icy wind was whipping off the Fens, but when I arrived at his house he was standing outside in the street, stripped to the waist and wearing only jodhpurs and riding boots and polishing a saddle. He told me that he had just got back from exercising his stallion. He still had the moustache but his hair had turned silver. And now there he was, large as life, mad as a snake, and a born-again Christian. When we were inside, the front door closed, he took me in his arms and said, 'I've been dreaming about you for years. When I heard your voice on the radio, I knew we were meant to be together.'

I pushed him away and said, 'You never seemed very keen at the time.'

'Ah,' he said, 'but I was young and foolish. Now I know what I need and it is you.'

That was enough. I left and never went back but, one day, after I had failed to return his calls or to answer his letters, he stormed into my Cambridge office, which was just around the corner from his house, and demanded to see me. This time, over his jodhpurs, he was wearing a crimson three-quarter-length coat with frogging and epaulettes and he was brandishing a riding crop. The men in the office persuaded him to leave quietly but this was by no means easy.

Half-way through the spring term, I fell in love with an American actor and this brought to an end, at least for the time being, my restlessness and promiscuity. This affair merits detailed description because it differed from all the others, both previous and subsequent, in that it contained an element of stability, of grown-upness.

Jerome, my boyfriend, was a member of a theatre group which had been formed by a man called Joe in California, in San Quentin prison. When Joe was nineteen, he had driven the car in a gas-station hold-up. The robbers had abducted the gas-station clerk; in an ensuing struggle, the clerk had been shot in the arm. At the time – or so Joe claimed – the only precedent in the state of California for kidnapping with violence was a lunatic who had kidnapped a pair of young lovers, then done terrible things to them. As a result, Joe was sentenced to life imprisonment without possibility of parole.

In San Quentin, Joe began to perform in and direct some of Samuel Beckett's plays. He developed what he called 'the San Quentin Beckett cycle', consisting of *Endgame*, *Waiting For Godot* and *Happy Days*. Beckett's plays, for obvious reasons, were thought to have a particular appeal among prisoners. Joe also wrote a play called *The Cage*, which was about prison life. Some critics came from San Francisco to see it as well as the Beckett cycle. They were hugely impressed, and one of them started a campaign to have Joe's sentence commuted to life with possibility of parole. Her cause was successful: Joe was granted parole, was released and married his critic benefactor.

None of the other actors in the group had been in prison – or not for more than a night. There were four of them – Joe, Jerome, a black guy called Curtis and Bob, who was English – and there was Joe's girlfriend, Lola.

Lola was eighteen years old, three years younger than me, a lush, Puerto Rican beauty with huge, dark eyes, black hair tumbling over her shoulders and a body like a *Playboy* centrefold. Joe was in his early forties and he was obsessed with her. When she was only fourteen and still living in Puerto Rico, she had run away from home with her boyfriend. Her father had called the police, then gone looking for them. In the confusion and struggle that followed, one of the policemen had shot and killed her father. Lola had had to leave the island.

Meanwhile, Joe's marriage to the theatre critic was in trouble; and as soon as he saw – only *saw* – Lola, he ran off with her. When I met them, they had been together for three years. They were a wild pair, gypsies, misfits if you like, outsiders certainly, and their individual tragedies bound them together. They made a striking couple; Lola, so young and with a beauty so vivid that it stunned, and Joe, bearded, grizzled, with a covertly menacing presence. On stage, he often forget or jumbled his lines, even the lines he had written himself, but somehow he always carried it off.

Jerome and I became lovers almost as soon as we met. I had never met anyone like him. He was apparently wholly at ease with himself, a grown-up. He was dark, muscular and had dark, curly hair on his chest. He came to live with me. I had moved again and lived in a big flat opposite the hospital where I had a big bedroom with a fireplace surrounded by Art Nouveau tiles with a design of lilies. There was no central heating; at night we would light the fire and lie in bed watching the flames. I bought an antique brass bed and painted the walls white and the woodwork black. I gave up my studies and dropped out of university. Jerome said I could be the theatre group's stage manager.

So began a rather wonderful period. I had a boyfriend who claimed, without reservation, to love me, and he showed it. I had a home. I had a job, or a sort of job (the group had no money so I didn't get paid). And I had friends. A woman called Nancy who wrote short stories and poems and had worked with Lindsay Kemp on his stage version of Genet's novel, *Our Lady of the Flowers*, had come to live with us. She had a baby boy called Lucien, and no husband or live-in boyfriend. Lucien was about a year old and cute as a button.

Nancy herself was an old-style bohemian, surrounding herself with actors, musicians, poets, aspiring novelists and assorted dead-beats, all of whom would traipse in and out of the apartment at all hours of the day and night. She had sparse red hair, hennaed, inexpertly permed and distributed over her skull like the feathers of a baby bird; she wore round glasses and had a short, dumpy body. Nonetheless, she had great style. She identified with – or modelled herself on – Stevie Smith, Billie Holiday and Juliette Greco. Now that I had thrown away my university career in favour of the theatre, I was free to devote myself to bohemian life too. Nancy was the perfect companion.

In the mornings we would spend hours in 1930s silk dressing gowns which we had bought in second-hand shops. We would sit in the kitchen of that icy flat drinking coffee, planning glamorous lives and discussing men and the trouble they brought. Nancy told me that her cunt felt like the Mersey Tunnel and wanted to know if there was sex after childbirth. There was – as she discovered some months later with a scrawny jazz musician. Nancy was also particularly keen on Jean Rhys; she saw herself, in some ways, as a Rhys character – abandoned by the father of her child, eking out a bohemian existence, alone against the world – but she was more of a survivor and had a more robust sense of humour than any of Rhys's tragic heroines. She said that she wanted the words: 'She never had a future, but Lordy, what a past!' carved on her tombstone

Stage managing felt like a poor substitute for the real thing. I was desperate to act – or, more accurately – to be an actress. I got my chance when Lola, who was playing Nell in *Endgame*, became pregnant and grew too fat to get into the barrel. Joe decided to let me have a go.

Lola's baby, a tiny, black-haired boy whom they named Raoul, was born shortly before we were due to go on tour. The group had been booked for a week by the state theatre in Berlin, to perform *The Cage* and *Endgame* on alternate nights. After Berlin, we were to go to Paris where Beckett was apparently coming to see us in his own play. It wasn't clear whether Lola or I would be on stage for the crucial Beckett performance and I didn't feel that I could ask Joe. I went south to London a couple of days before the others. Ralph was there; the night before the troupe left for Berlin, we slept together.

Despite the fact that sex had entered the picture, the pattern of my relationship with Ralph had not really altered since my schooldays when he was my friend's glamorous, elder brother. I was still always trying to get him to notice me, to pay attention to me. His reluctance to do so in any significant way guaranteed my continuing interest. He must have known it would. Looking back, it was, it now seems, inevitable that even a stable, contented, sexually fulfilling relationship with a man who loved me would be no match for my doomed craving for Ralph. Matters were further complicated by my sense that Ralph somehow belonged to the real world, my real world. True, it was a world in which I was unhappy, paranoid, freaked-out and fickle, but that didn't seem to matter as much as the fact that I felt real, like *me*, rather than a stranger in a cocoon of domesticity. Sex with Jerome was easy; he would touch me and I would come. Boom. With Ralph, I felt my spirit move, or thought I did, and that seemed more important, certainly more interesting. Good sex – my version of it – was like drowning, terrifying but slow. Ralph approached love-making like a surgeon, his hands as delicate and cruel as I could wish.

Jerome arrived by plane from Edinburgh the next morning. We went to have lunch in an open-air restaurant in Leicester Square before leaving for Germany. My heart and mind were full of Ralph and I could hardly hear, let alone comprehend, what Jerome was saying. He had been, I suppose, talking about us, our *future*, for some minutes when suddenly he said – and this I heard loud and clear – 'Will you marry me?' I have no idea what I answered, but that evening, on the night train to Berlin, Jerome told me that I had looked completely horrified at his proposal.

In Berlin it always seemed to be night-time. Jerome and I were staying with a musician called Horst and his girlfriend, Birgid, in a flat above a bar. After the show we would go to meet them wherever Horst was playing and sit up drinking with them and their musician friends, playing poker until the early hours. Often we stopped off at the bar downstairs for one last schnapps. Then we would all stagger back to the flat and sleep for most of the day till it was time for us to leave for the theatre.

Jerome and I slept on a mattress on a sort of gallery platform next to the hot water tank above the bathroom and, in the time between waking and working, would make love in a desperate, anxious, intensely sexual way. I felt guilty about betraying Jerome. He sensed my betrayal, without knowing the details, and his pain fuelled his passion for me. I daydreamed endlessly about Ralph (the time in the barrel just flew); Jerome, aware of my abstraction, tried desperately to woo me back to the present with his caresses.

One night I had a dream about Ralph. I dreamt that I was staying in the big house in the country with them all. Ralph, looking very smart, rushed past on his way out to work. He didn't speak to me. I went after him and kissed him. 'Oh, don't start that,' he said.

'Telephone me,' I said.

He answered, 'That'll be the day, that'll be the day . . .'

'That I die,' I said.

Horst was a big, fat man with a straggly ponytail; he had done seven years in prison in Spain for stabbing to death a man who had gone off with his girlfriend. The experience hadn't made him bitter but it did make one think twice about crossing him. He and Joe got on fine. There was a natural kinship between them; they had both spent time on the wrong side of the tracks. Birgid, with her rosy apple cheeks and shiny black hair cut in a bob, looked just like a Dutch doll. It clearly wasn't easy living with Horst and after a few days she began sleeping with Bob in the afternoons, when Horst was rehearsing or seeing his friends. I dreaded to think what would happen if Horst found out.

Meanwhile, relations between Jerome and myself and Joe and Lola were increasingly strained. Joe wanted Lola back playing Nell again and expected me to look after the baby during performances. I didn't see why I should – he wasn't *my* baby. I couldn't stand to hear him cry so I would leave the theatre during the show. Lola couldn't bear his crying either and her performance suffered as a result. One evening Raoul screamed so loudly that he could be heard in the foyer. Everybody was worried about money and what was going to happen after Paris. We were making a loss in Berlin, even though the houses were good, and there were no more bookings. I overheard Jerome saying to the German box-office manager, 'I can't send these people home without a penny.' Joe was muddling his lines worse than ever, which drove Jerome crazy. Joe and Lola quarrelled about whether she should play Nell or look after the baby. Curtis, who had been ill before we left Edinburgh and had been given every test in the book, wasn't getting any better; he was losing weight and ached all over. 'He's got syphilis,' I said, but he had been tested for that. Jerome and I fuckèd like rabbits and had almost stopped speaking to each other. I still loved him, felt comfortable and safe with him, but I was obsessed with Ralph. I didn't know what I was going to do. The future was too terrifying to contemplate.

One night, as usual, we came back to the flat late. It was after three but the bar downstairs was still open, a light glowing dimly from inside. I peered through the frosted glass and saw that it had just one customer, a small, thin, old man, who was usually there; he was the admirer of Gerta, the proprietress, an overblown blonde in her fifties, twice his size. The scene reminded me of a painting by Edward Hopper, seediness and loneliness frozen in time.

We went in for a drink. Gerta fancied Jerome; she would light up like a neon sign whenever she saw him. That night, when the jukebox began to play 'Viva España', she came out from behind the bar and asked him to dance. They began a spirited polka. The old boy got off his bar-stool and held out his hand to me. The four of us whirled round and round the room, faster and faster, as if on an out of control merry-go-round. With each chorus of 'Eh, Viva España', the old man would stop to stamp his feet, click his heels and clap his hands above his head. Suddenly, mid-twirl, he slipped on the polished floor and fell heavily. As he did so, something – it looked like a piece of raw liver – shot out of his mouth and under one of the tables pushed back against the wall.

When the run in Berlin was finished, we took the night train to Paris, arriving early in the morning at the Gare du Nord. Jerome went to the lavatory and came back to tell us that a man had been masturbating at the urinal next to him. I hadn't slept at all and was almost hallucinating with fatigue. I couldn't walk straight. The pavements dipped and swayed as if I was on board ship. We made our way to the theatre where we were to perform; then Joe went to telephone Beckett.

There were to be just four performances of *Endgame*

in Paris; we had no idea which one, if any, Beckett would attend. Joe and I had reached a sort of truce. Lola and I would each do two shows and I would take care of the baby while she was on stage. Joe was anxious that Lola should be performing when Beckett came. I was equally anxious that *I* should be. It was a bit like having a lottery ticket and waiting to see who had won. In the end, nobody won. Beckett never came. Ralph had said that he wouldn't.

Fourteen

I returned to England alone. Christmas was just five days away. Jerome and the others stayed on in Paris to meet Beckett. That, at least, happened. Somewhere I still have some photographs of Jerome with the great man.

At home my parents were cautiously pleased to see me; they treated me increasingly as if I was an unpredictable animal who might at any moment bite or contract a rare and incurable illness. That year my father's Christmas card to me bore a photograph of a scowling, blonde girl weighed down by a couple of large suitcases, all her worldly possessions. Inside he had written: 'To my darling, wayward daughter, with love from Daddy'. They both wondered out loud what I was going to do now. So did I. Jerome had been talking more and more about returning to America in the new year, even though the group had received a definite offer to perform *Endgame* in London. Lola was pregnant again; if Jerome were to stay, there might after all be another chance for me in the barrel (in the end, Joe and Lola went back to Berlin to put on *Waiting For Godot*; there Lola had an abortion).

But Jerome was fed up with Joe and Lola and the chaotic way in which they – and the group – operated. Above all he was tired of being short of money. He wanted to leave and he wanted me to go to California with him. In spite of everything Jerome still loved me but I couldn't imagine living with him in Los Angeles. I pictured us living in a small, shabby house in a vast, sprawling suburb, a house which would look just like every other house for miles around, a house in a row in a street that looked like every other street.

In my fantasy I would have to stay at home in this house and I wouldn't know anybody. I didn't want to be a housewife and I assumed that was what I would be. I don't know why I thought that – something to do with cooking I guess. Jerome and I were always arguing about whose turn it was to cook. I didn't much like cooking then, probably because I wasn't any good at it; I hated the whole ritual of food preparation and then eating, the tyranny of meals, the way we had – seemingly – to eat at the same time each day: breakfast, lunch, dinner, day after day. We couldn't afford to go out. When I think of it now, my agitation seems absurd. I suppose my reluctance to cook, to learn to cook, was a legacy from the years of school meals and servants at home. I had never had to cook before, so I didn't see why I had to now. Or perhaps – and actually this seems more likely – it was a fear of settling down to what I imagined would be a suburban, regulated existence. Cooking – domesticity – seemed suffocating. Jerome pointed out that I was happy enough to eat whenever he had cooked. It was true. But whenever it was my turn to cook, I didn't want to and would say that I wasn't hungry.

I have often tried to work out what Jerome saw in me. I was difficult and unfaithful and prone to tantrums and great selfish waves of insecurity. Jerome wasn't a masochist; he was a grown man and his willingness to put up with all this was puzzling – and faintly despicable. I guess that he loved me. I have always had problems accepting love when it has been offered. I want it so much and then when it comes, I don't know how to deal with it.

Also, again, I could think of nothing but Ralph. I spent hours brooding about him – obsessively repeating his name like an incantation, as if the repetition would magically bestow on our relationship – such as it was – the promise of a blissful future.

I waged constant bets with myself about the likelihood of Ralph's telephoning me. I fantasized about a camping holiday for two with *one* sleeping bag. In such choice circumstances, he would come to know and love me. I made special pilgrimages from Oxford to London – which I could ill afford – in the hope of seeing him. Sometimes I succeeded; sometimes we met and went to bed. This made everything at first better, then much worse. When we made love, Ralph's tenderness would almost bring tears to my eyes; be still my heart. How could we make love as we did and not love each other? It had to mean something. Now I think that I was probably right; it did mean *something*. But it wasn't something which he was prepared to acknowledge, let alone cultivate; in the morning, he would behave as if we were strangers. In the one serious conversation we had, he said, 'Perhaps this is how our relationship is meant to be: arguments, silences, sleeping together and then not seeing each other for three months.' I'm not so sure that it was how our relationship was *meant* to be. It was certainly how it *was*.

Mostly he would be impossibly offhand. Sometimes he wouldn't ring at all and I would be reduced to telephoning him late at night and hanging up when I heard his voice. One night I rang him drunk from a callbox. He answered, sounding sleepy, and I hung up, only to ring again half an hour later just to wake him again. Then I thought, 'Oh God, perhaps he has a girl there and he's telling her there is this crazy girl who keeps pursuing him.'

Fleur reported that Ralph had a steady girlfriend and that 'no doubt was why he was rather cool'. He may indeed have had a steady girlfriend but he wasn't faithful to her. At moments like this, I felt quite desperate, quite mad – I wanted to die, to cut my throat or my wrists. Jerome seemed a beacon of sanity; it was imperative that he didn't leave England and me. I didn't believe that I would ever see him again if he left.

A couple of weeks into the new year Jerome and I went back up to Edinburgh. Jerome had decided definitely to return to California and planned to leave in a few weeks. He said that he would send for me. I said that I would come. We made promises – which, deep down, in our hearts, neither of us can really have believed. Everything in Edinburgh seemed unreal. Curtis was in hospital. The doctors had finally succeeded in diagnosing his illness. It was syphilis – just as I had guessed. Curtis was bisexual and very attractive. He had had a number of lovers in the city, male and female. They all had to be notified and some of them hospitalized. The male ones were put in the same ward with him. It should have been embarrassing but somehow it was funny – the only thing that *was* funny that bleak January.

As the date for Jerome's departure drew nearer, my behaviour grew worse and worse. I would stay out till all hours, often with other men. Men for whom I cared nothing – whom I didn't love and who didn't love me. Jerome said nothing. He took it all with an immense, weary patience. Perhaps he knew that I was hurting myself at least as much as I was hurting him.

The night after Jerome flew off to Los Angeles and the night before I was due to leave Edinburgh for good, Nancy went out on a date. She hadn't been to bed with anyone since Lucien was born and was both longing for and dreading sex. She thought tonight might be the night. I stayed home and baby-sat with Alec, an old friend of Nancy's who was staying with us for a few days, sleeping on the big, old, green sofa in the living-room. We were sitting up in front of the fire, talking and drinking whisky, when Nancy arrived home, rosy-cheeked, bright-eyed, slightly drunk. She had brought her date, a skinny jazz musician with a straggly goatee, back with her. She was pleased as Punch with her catch, wearing him on her arm like a bracelet. They sat around for a few minutes; then they went to bed.

They could scarcely have pulled off their clothes before the baby began to cry. He slept in a big walk-in cupboard that linked my room to the sitting-room. An alarm had been wired up to Nancy's room so that she could hear Lucien if he cried; within minutes, she came running, half-naked, struggling into her pink silk Art Deco kimono. She and the musician had been just about to make sweet music. She picked the baby up, cuddled him till he stopped crying and then put him back down to sleep. Fifteen minutes later the same thing happened. Mothers are supposed to have a sixth sense where their babies are concerned. Maybe babies have it too.

The third time it happened, I said, 'If he cries again, I'll get him. Go back to bed and enjoy yourself. Don't worry.'

Lucien cried again within minutes and I got up and took him into the sitting-room. Alec was awake and we played with the child till he fell asleep exhausted in my arms. Alec looked at me over Lucien and then he leant across and kissed me.

I took the baby and laid him down in his cot. He was sleeping sweetly now. Like a baby. Then I went back to my room and climbed into bed with Alec.

When I think back to that night, it seems typical of so much of that period of my life. I liked Alec well enough, though I hardly knew him. But I didn't fancy him at all, had never consciously, even for a minute, thought of him in a sexual way. (I don't think I knew how to relate to men except sexually – since, even if they weren't being sexual, I was.) Alec wasn't good-looking; his face, even his body, was sort of bulbous. Everything about him was misshapen and clumsy but he was a nice man. He had had a youthful marriage – to a model or an actress – which had gone wrong and left him sad and slightly lost. I was slightly lost too. Despite my lack of desire for him – or perhaps because of it – we spent an oddly passionate night together, hardly pausing, between our couplings, to sleep.

This wasn't the first time something like this had happened and I imagined that it wouldn't be the last. I didn't try to analyse why such things came about; I just accepted them as a part of the way life was. My life. Men you didn't fancy fancied you; men you fancied didn't fancy you, or sometimes only for a night or two. Men you loved – or thought you loved – didn't love you back and men who loved you felt compelled to get on planes which took them thousands of miles away.

But one thing I had worked out was this: that there were lots of boys who tried it on with lots of girls and they were bound to get lucky some of the time. And if, like me, you were thought beautiful, you would get asked a lot and if, also like me, you were bad at saying 'No', you would end up kissing and even fucking many of the wrong men while searching for the right one. And sometimes, paradoxically, you would enjoy it with one of the wrong men while it was actually going on, even if afterwards you hated him, and yourself even more. It was hard enough to enjoy the whole business of sex when you knew your mother thought you were a slut for doing it – and when you feared that she might be right. Harder still when you were doing it with a man or a boy you didn't fancy and to whom you had been trying – albeit, it would appear, with total lack of success - to say 'No.' *No.* NO.

But that was the way it was and there didn't seem to be a lot I could do to change it.

Early the next morning I met Nancy in the kitchen. She was smiling.

'Well,' she said, 'so I wasn't the only one to have a good time last night.'

I could feel myself blushing.

'What do you mean?'

'Oh, come on. You can't have got a wink's sleep.'

It turned out that she had forgotten to turn down the volume on the baby alarm. The sounds of Alec's and my love-making had filtered through to the baby's cupboard and had been broadcast to Nancy and her musician all night long. I was mortified. Somehow the fact that I hadn't fancied Alec (though I could hardly expect Nancy to believe that now), yet had still flung myself into the night with gusto, made it all worse.

Later that day I left Edinburgh for good. My mother had driven up from Oxford in a big station-wagon and we loaded all my belongings into it. The brass bed came too, lashed to the roof-rack. Alec helped us load the car. I never saw him again and about a year later he died – or killed himself – falling, or jumping, from an open window. Even Nancy, who had been close to Alec and known him for many years, could never decide whether his death was an accident or suicide.

I never saw Jerome again either. For about six or maybe nine months after he left, he wrote to me – devoted, practical letters on thin blue airmail paper in which he talked about looking for work and a place to live and when we would be together again. Letters about money, time and distance. For a period, we conspired to sustain the myth that it was just a matter of time before I went to America to join him. Then the letters stopped. I don't know why. I don't think that I ever wrote to tell him that I definitely wasn't going to join him. I don't think that I ever knew that I definitely wasn't going to. But I suppose he must eventually have guessed and then decided to get on with his life. After the letters stopped coming I only once had news of him – through a friend of his called Larry.

Larry, a short man who looked a bit like Woody Allen,

was a Californian photographer who had hung around the theatre group in Edinburgh. He had come to Berlin with us and had taken the photographs of Jerome with Samuel Beckett. He wrote to me from Venice a few months after Jerome had gone back to Los Angeles. I had always suspected that he was interested in me but his letter spelt it out. He wrote,

> One situation I have always found to be painful and generally self-destructive is the third party in a 2 person relationship . . . I don't wish to become that 3rd party, but would like to maintain communication with you that would not necessarily involve Jerome. I am not looking for anything more than a chance to get to know you without Jerome. I somehow sensed there are things about our lives that would be enjoyable to communicate but are personal enough not to necessarily be shared. Do I make myself understandable? I hope so.

I didn't answer. Five years later, he wrote to me again, to tell me that he was coming to London. This second letter was long, filling me in (his phrase) on what he had been doing since we last met.

> I've been evolving a complex form of collage that integrates my photographs and many other visual sources . . . I also wrote two screenplays (none sold unfortunately). The first was about a woman reporter and I hoped that you wouldn't mind but I named her after you . . .

When he arrived, we had dinner at an Indian restaurant and Larry told me that Jerome was working, that he had a girlfriend who was an actress. Then he made a pass at me. This was, I suppose, inevitable. He said that he had always fancied me. I felt sure that this was true, but I also think that, in some way, he fancied Jerome, or envied him; he wanted whatever Jerome had or had once had. Seeing him only made me feel nostalgic for Jerome and all that I had lost or rejected; I told him that I wasn't interested.

I have never been to Los Angeles, except once to the airport, on a stopover on the way to Hawaii. But I have friends there who always say 'You must come, you'd love it', and sometimes I have fantasies about arriving in LA and looking Jerome up in the telephone book and calling him. Whenever I see an American movie, I look for his name in the credits, in the small letters, among the bit-part actors. I never find it; sometimes I see actors on the screen who remind me of him, occasionally even to the extent that I think, 'Oh, that's him. That's Jerome', but it never is. It never is him.

Nor have I ever again seen or heard from any other members of the group. I don't know if Joe and Lola are still together, if Joe is back in prison, if they had another baby, even if they are alive or if they're dead. Another closed chapter of my life, a part of it that seems only to have happened in dream time.

Fifteen

After Jerome left, I went to live, for what turned out to be six months, with my brother and sister in a tall, narrow house in Oxford which backed on to the canal. I got a job as a waitress in a French restaurant down the road from our house. The restaurant was run by a grumpy Pole who made us hand over all our tips to him. I mainly worked the lunch shift which left me free to party in the evening. And party I did. This world was entirely different from Edinburgh, or from that of the theatre. It was bright and glittery, full of money and privilege and ease. A world of stately homes and family retainers, of fast, expensive cars and villas in Italy or Spain, of fashionable night-clubs like Annabel's or Tramp. I saw it as a sort of Martini world, full of beautiful people. The boys were all called Jasper, Caspar, Peregrine, Rupert, Edward or Sebastian; they were tall and handsome and wore blue jeans and velvet jackets in rich purples and crimsons with floppy cravats. The girls – Arabella, Janey, Joanna, Charlotte, Camilla, Flora, Melissa and Emma – all seemed to be blonde, clad in long, flowery dresses. The fashion at the time was for printed chiffon, the soft, faded colours of old roses and no underwear. The second-hand clothes shops in Edinburgh had been full of these dresses, left over from the 1930s when they had first been in vogue, incredibly fragile and gossamer-thin. I had collected quite a few of them then and in Oxford used to spend hours carefully mending the tears and frayed seams before setting forth to dazzle the world.

Here I was suddenly surrounded by money. In this society, it was taken for granted that the boys would pay. Nobody had heard of going Dutch, or if they had, it hadn't caught on; this meant that boys like Louis (who I re-encountered in Oxford) and my brother, who didn't have private incomes or trust funds, found themselves having to spend every penny of their allowances on taking girls to restaurants. Quite often these were girls they barely knew, because if a group of, say, ten went out to dinner, the boys automatically divided the bill between them.

I wondered about this as we sat around having conversations about the total impossibility, darling, of surviving on less than £50 a week (in Edinburgh I had lived on £9 a week, dole money). But I was the only one to be concerned. My first (and only) boyfriend in Oxford, whose eyebrows met above the bridge of his nose and whose big, brown irises floated strangely in a sea of white, had more money than sense. I soon learnt to take his largesse for granted.

One evening, in his house, we all took LSD. I was, in the main, uninterested in drugs, except for marijuana and LSD which I had first tried in Richmond Park with Fleur and a boy called Nigel who went on to become a famous comic actor. I enjoyed acid, the truth drug – it was so interesting – but it decimated you. You needed days to recover. I only took it twice in all the years in Edinburgh. Damon had had no interest in it: it required too much energy for him.

This time I spent the whole night lying on a bed upstairs with a pretty, gay boy who looked like a big-eyed, long-lashed girl, bitching about the people we knew. It seemed poetic as we lay beneath an open window gazing up at the night sky, counting the stars, seeing the faces of the gods in the clouds, awestruck at the purity, the deep blueness of the heavens. Acid does that. You can't believe the colours. And nature. Oh, isn't nature wonderful? But acid truths are self-evident and when the drug wore off, all I was left with was the realization that my life was empty and shallow. I missed Nancy and Lucien. I missed Jerome. I hated the way I seemed to be able to move on, slippery as a snake, leaving no traces behind me and taking nothing with me from the past. The things that had mattered so desperately, the people I had cared for – Damon, Jerome and the others – I had simply lost, or discarded along the way, like so much baggage. I had no continuity; the past closed behind me like the waters of the Red Sea.

When, after six months, I moved to London, I still had dreams of becoming an actress, but they gradually withered and died after I failed to get into drama school. I took a job teaching English to foreign businessmen and started to sniff vast quantities of amphetamine sulphate (poor man's cocaine) to help me get through the day and keep boredom at bay. And I watched, eager as a puppy, helpless as a baby, the progress of my affair with Ralph.

I couldn't acknowledge this at the time but there wouldn't have been an affair if it weren't for me. All the impetus was mine. My longing and determination kept the whole thing going as if the relationship were an accident victim and my love the respirator which kept it breathing. If ever I were to give up, to abandon hope, to relax even for a minute, it would die. I was the life support machine that kept it alive. But, unexpectedly, it was given a new lease of life.

In London I had gone to live in a former artist's studio in Chelsea belonging to an old boyfriend called Conrad. I had met Conrad during my last summer in Athens. He was the son of a famous (dead) writer of spy thrillers and a legendary bitch and beauty who had visited the embassy for a few days; Conrad and I had clambered over the perimeter fence in order to visit the Parthenon in the moonlight and had been caught by the police. I told them that I was the daughter of the British Ambassador and we were escorted home in a police car. Once back, we stayed up all night talking and eventually went to bed together in the early hours. It wasn't a success but I was too inexperienced to notice; he wasn't, however, and his failure never ceased to rankle with him.

Conrad's studio had been built at the turn of the century and contained a vast, beautiful room, two storeys high, with huge, crenellated windows through which sunlight flooded. The house was on the corner of the street; its windows faced south-west and south-east and the sun, when there was sun, poured into the studio all day long. There wasn't much furniture, just two long white sofas that faced each other, a couple of low lamps and a stereo system. As the shadows lengthened at dusk and night arrived in the studio, the far corners of the room vanished in the darkness. Once all trace of the day had gone, I'd close the tall wooden shutters and switch on the lamps on the floor. My friends and I would lie on the sofas and on the floor, stoned, looking up at the soft circles of light on the high, high ceiling and listening to the kind of trippy music that we favoured at the time: the Incredible String Band, Syd Barrett, John McLaughlin, all exotic string and wind instruments influenced by the mystic east, with more than a touch of Celtic looniness. Sometimes the speed made me paranoid and I'd start hearing voices, imagining little enemies hiding in the shadows, whispering that I'd better watch out, *they* were coming to get me.

Apart from the glorious studio, the apartment had only a bathroom and, in the basement, a gloomy, little-used kitchen with a sunless, tiled patio out back where a few pot plants straggled, then died. My bedroom, across the corridor from the kitchen, was a narrow, boring room with a single bed. Conrad slept in a strange sort of *oubliette*, like a priest's hole, up a ladder near the front door, where he had extended a large mattress. I only went up there twice during the entire eight months that I lived in his studio.

I loved that apartment, particularly when Conrad, who was now a registered drug addict and in and out of mental hospitals and clean-up clinics, wasn't there and I was the queen of my kingdom. Ralph liked it too. He would turn up, usually unannounced, late in the evening, often on the run from a gay director or actor whom he would have encouraged almost to the point of no return (the Royal Court theatre was just up the road). Sometimes he would bring his suitor with him and I would be paraded as his girlfriend, tangible evidence of his heterosexuality and unavailability.

One evening shortly before eleven o'clock, the doorbell

rang. There, standing on the doorstep, was Ralph, beautiful and sluttish in a black velvet jacket and ripped jeans; beside him, his hands twisting nervously, was a middle-aged man whose sad, baggy face I recognized. He was a theatre director and quite well known; his production of Joe Orton's *Entertaining Mr Sloane* was playing at the Royal Court. They came in and I went downstairs to fetch drinks. Ralph followed me into the kitchen and began to kiss me, thrusting his tongue into my mouth, backing me up against the fridge and pulling my skirt up around my waist. Still entangled, our ankles meshing like cogs, we crossed the corridor to my bedroom and fell on to the bed, Ralph unzipping his jeans on the way. As we made love – if you can call it that – I could hear the director pacing in the studio above. The knowledge that his admirer was upstairs – waiting, wondering, humiliated – excited Ralph. Of that I am sure. Ten minutes later when we sauntered back, rosy and sated, Ralph had a complacent, possessive smile on his lips. He had made his point.

Towards the end of the summer I went to spend a weekend with Conrad and Katherine, his mother, in the country, where they lived in a large, elegant, grey stone, eighteenth-century house with a wonderful cook and every comfort. I had been there many times before, but I never managed to enjoy myself. Katherine was a complicated, sophisticated woman, famous for her glittering parties, her cruel wit and her dark beauty: since the death of Conrad's father, her third husband, she had had many admirers and lovers. (Conrad claimed to have seen her kissing my father in the garden of the embassy in Athens

– I could never decide if he was telling the truth but the thought of it made me feel uneasy: certainly she never had a good word for my mother, saying once, in the most dismissive terms, 'Yes, we *all* know about your mother's difficulties with servants.') Conrad's father, Graham, was, I think, the great love of her life. A difficult, brilliant man, he had been a manic depressive and habitual user of Benzedrine. He had killed himself when Conrad was still a child.

Conrad was born when Katherine was in her mid forties. The adored son of her favourite husband, he had always been alarmingly precocious and intellectually complex. Almost from birth, she had treated him as an adult and an equal; after Graham's death, he became her boon companion. They enjoyed (perhaps 'enjoyed' isn't quite the right word) a love–hate relationship, behaving more like long-term lovers or characters out of *Who's Afraid of Virginia Woolf?* than like mother and son. Any guest was in danger of getting caught in the cross-fire. (Literally, sometimes: Conrad once fired a bow and arrow at me as I was climbing out of the swimming-pool; on another occasion, he aimed a Luger at me.) This time, he had implored me to come and he had promised to behave.

After dinner, the grown-ups, a distinguished, homosexual don from Oxford, and Katherine, went to bed. Conrad and I stayed up drinking Polish vodka and gossiping, lying side by side on the white fur rug in front of the fireplace under the portrait of Katherine by Lucian Freud. When he began to kiss me, it was for the first time in five years. We had had endless discussions about the past and what the future might hold for both of us but he had not touched me since that night in Athens. He began tentatively, then grew more ardent until suddenly, almost without my realizing it, half my clothes were on the rug and his hands were all over me. It was too late to object, even if I had wanted to, and I wasn't sure that I did: anyhow, I thought maybe, if it went well, it might help and then at least we could move on from the past.

Conrad had never recovered from what he perceived as the humiliation of that initial encounter. What we had done – climbing over the perimeter fence to wander around the Parthenon at midnight in the moonlight – was so romantic that for it to have been followed by impotence was more than he could bear. But his nature (together with his upbringing) had conspired to make it almost impossible for him to express his feelings: he was too clever (he thought himself far cleverer than any of the shrinks he saw and he had seen quite a few) and too damaged for normal life. Everything was coloured by irony and sarcasm. Nevertheless, I never doubted that he minded quite a lot about what had happened – or rather, what had not happened. For one thing, he brought it up again and again, as if it had been just yesterday.

We went upstairs to Conrad's room and began to make love in his single bed. It was a warm night and the curtains were open; moonlight shone through the window, illuminating the delicate ivy trellises that covered the façade of the house. Conrad was very thin and his bony hips dug into my thighs. I could just make out his expression, determined, anxious. At first all was fine but then it went on and on – for hours, it seemed. This time his problem was different and I knew exactly what it was. Conrad was taking so many drugs (mainly barbiturates, but also methadone and sometimes amphetamines) that he couldn't come. He began to hurt me and, eventually, even at the risk of upsetting him again, I had to ask him to stop. I was tired and sore. I went back to my own room and fell asleep.

The next morning at breakfast Conrad turned to me and said, 'So, miss, and how are you this morning?'

'Fine, thank you,' I said.

'Ooh, listen to her,' he said, looking round at his mother and the famous academic, his voice dripping with camp venom, as if he were Kenneth Williams. 'So cool. But I can tell you, she wasn't like this last night. You should have seen her! Lying in my arms! A real goer!'

I had seen Conrad like this before, spewing bile, as if the devil had got into him. But I couldn't wait to hear what would come next. I pushed back my chair and ran from the room. Katherine came after me and found me crying in the downstairs cloakroom.

'Don't pay any attention to him,' she said. 'You know it's the drugs'.

Of course, I did know it was the drugs, but I knew too that it was also Conrad's bitter unhappiness and loathing of life and his mother. I never went there again. I never slept with Conrad again. And, just days after that weekend, I moved out of the studio and went to live with a girlfriend in a dull, small flat in West Kensington.

By the end of the long, hot, steamy summer, Conrad had got worse, so ill that he had to be committed. His doctors diagnosed 'malignant depression'. He rang me from a callbox in the asylum, begging me to get him out somehow. But it was clear that there was nothing I could do. Katherine sold the studio. A couple of months later,

Conrad, who had been released from his hospital, came to have lunch with me near the language school where I taught. He was wearing a long-sleeved, blue cotton shirt and had rolled up the sleeves to his elbows. I saw that the insides of his forearms were covered with track marks. He had never injected drugs before – that is, not as far as I was aware.

Horrified, I asked him to roll down his sleeves. He refused: he appeared almost proud of the marks, sporting them like a kind of badge of honour or battle scars. He seemed wilder, more desperate than ever before. He had a new girlfriend, whom I knew, and knew to be a heroin addict.

I never saw Conrad again. He drowned himself in the Caribbean, where he had gone for a therapeutic holiday after the break-up of his relationship with the addict. One evening, around sunset, he swallowed a handful of barbiturates and then swam out to sea. His suicide note said simply, 'If it is not this time, it will be the next. Please give my collection [of antiquities] to the Pitt-Rivers Museum.' His body was flown back to England and his funeral was held near his mother's country house. I didn't go. I pretended to myself that I couldn't take time off work. I could have, of course, and as soon as I had decided not to go and once the funeral was over, I regretted my decision. I still do. But it's too late now.

Ralph got a job as an assistant director at a theatre in the north of England. He was delighted, of course. I was devastated, and his failure to reassure me that it would make no difference to us only served to emphasize just what a difference it would make. As it was, our honeymoon was all but over.

When the end came with Ralph, it came swiftly and dramatically, like a thunderstorm, or an aneurism, apparently without warning.

A week or so before he left for Leeds, there was a party in Kensington to celebrate the twenty-first birthday of a pair of pretty, blonde, twin heiresses. Gallons of champagne and a professional discotheque. The older men were wearing dinner jackets. Ralph and I had come separately but had arranged to leave together. At some point during the evening, I wandered across the dance floor and found Ralph slow-dancing, cheek-to-cheek with a slender, dark-haired girl. Her name was Ronnie, short for Veronica; she was a friend of one of his younger sisters. He was kissing her on the mouth. I put my hand on his shoulder. He turned to face me and I slapped him. Then I walked across the room to a marble side-table on which trays of champagne flutes were arranged. I began to pick up the glasses, one by one, and throw them on to the parquet floor. They shattered as they landed.

Ralph came over to where I was standing surrounded by broken glass. I must have broken at least twenty glasses. Tears rained down my cheeks.

He collected my coat and we walked all the way home. It was about two in the morning, the end of a warm, hazy evening. Half-way there I sat down on the pavement and said, 'It's over, isn't it?'

'Yes,' said Ralph, 'Yes, it is.'

When we got back to the flat, I made some tea and then we went to bed and made love with a sweet, slow sadness, knowing that it was to be the last time.

Part Three

The women sleep.
We look for them in their dreams.

When we bump into a piece of scenery,
It falls, waking them.

They open eyes full of broken love.
Love that we have broken.

from 'Broken Dreams' by Hugo Williams

Sixteen

That night was over twenty years ago. I love the sound of breaking glass; I hate it if I actually break anything. So I take empty bottles in their dozens to the recycling dump and listen to them smash, secure in the knowledge that I am doing good, not harm.

It took me some time, some years, to accept that it was over, and still more years and several other lovers before I could bear to see Ralph with another woman without feeling physically sick. At one point, because of this obsession, I literally nearly killed myself.

One summer afternoon I saw Ralph with a beautiful brunette at a garden party in Little Venice. I drank too many glasses of Pimm's, snorted a couple of lines of amphetamine sulphate and drove off. A few streets away I misjudged a turn, skidded – my car tyres were almost bald – and ploughed into a crash barrier somewhere near the beginning of the M40 flyover. The police, the ambulance services and the fire brigade all turned out in my honour. I wasn't hurt – only, as they say, shocked and bruised – but I was that already. The car was a wreck. I was lucky to survive. They took me to the police station, breathalysed me and found that I was way over the limit. The drugs didn't show up in the blood test.

When I appeared in court some months later, charged with drunk driving, my solicitor told the judge, 'My client is very sorry. She had been at a party where she saw one of her ex-fiancés with another woman and she was so upset that she drank too much.'

The judge wasn't impressed. 'Exactly how many ex-fiancés does your client have?' he asked dryly, before fining me £200 and disqualifying me from driving for eighteen months.

Ralph married a sulky, black-haired actress who looked so much like him that she could have been his sister and they had four little, black-haired children, each one looking just like the other and just like their parents, as if they had been cloned rather than conceived. He had met his wife when he directed her in a hugely successful television adaption of a cult novel about beautiful people at Oxford. It was almost as if he were directing an adaption of his own life.

Ralph's early promise had, in fact, failed to materialize and, with the fading of his youthful radiance, followed by his marriage, his appeal diminished. The last I heard, he was directing commercials. Commercials! Now when I see him at parties – which I do once every two or three years – I don't feel a thing: not a pang, not a flicker. He is friendly, middle-aged and a little paunchy. He looks now as his father did at the same age. He reminds me of Alan Bates. All the early, dazzling beauty has gone. I suspect that he has fond memories of the past and of me. Why shouldn't he?

Twenty years ago Fleur got married. She had broken up with Sean while she was still at Cambridge, met someone else there and married him soon after graduating. She had a white wedding in a big, fashionable, Roman Catholic church. Her husband is a good man, nice, decent; they live in a ramshackle house in the country, subscribe to various New Age beliefs and have five children. I am godmother to the second youngest. She is a girl with a free and wanton spirit; I sometimes catch myself seeking to curb her. Fleur is my oldest, my favourite friend and I wish her nothing but good. Nevertheless I often find myself envying her: her fecundity, her beautiful children, her freedom from money worries, her faithful husband and regular sex. But I know that things are never quite as they seem.

I have lost touch with Nancy. About seven years after I left Edinburgh, she moved to Oxford to take a degree in Hebrew (in her thirties, she had rediscovered her Jewishness and become a practising Jew). She got a First. I last saw her in the Eighties, at Lucien's bar mitzvah. Eighteen months ago I tried the number I had for her in Oxford. The woman who answered the phone had never heard of Nancy or of Lucien.

Louis got married too. I don't know much about his life in the years between Oxford and the beginning of our affair, except what I was able to glean from things he has let slip. He graduated triumphantly, moved to London and set up house with Anna, his Oxford girlfriend. Somewhere along the line she left him. I don't know why – his drinking, I expect, or maybe an infidelity too far. She found out about the night we spent together on Valentine's Day (I imagine that he told her); her reaction, he says, was to tell him that he made her sick. But she didn't leave then; she stuck around for a couple more years. Now she's a countess, or maybe a marchioness, and the only woman for whom Louis never has a bad word.

Soon after Anna left him (very soon after, I think), Louis married. It seems to have happened very quickly. He was young; she was young, a pretty girl of good family. Everyone said they made a lovely couple, resplendent with promise and grace, their lives before them. I remember seeing the wedding pictures in *Tatler* and feeling a pang of envy: Emily, with her white teeth, cute, *retroussé* nose and aristocratic connections; Louis, with his brilliance and his beauty, both of them visibly glowing with the excitement of the day. But it didn't last, none of it did, not the marriage nor the promise.

'I never really loved her, you know,' Louis told me one night. 'On the morning of the wedding I was in a complete panic. It was just one of those things. I got caught up in it and before I knew where I was, there we were walking up the aisle. You know how it is.'

I didn't believe Louis when he said that he had never loved Emily. It was tempting to believe him when he told me that I was the only woman he had ever truly loved – the first and now the last – but of course I understand that love comes in many shades of grey and that the part played by hope or desperation should never be underestimated.

I married as well. That didn't last either. In fact, you could say – and several people, including my mother and father, did say – that my marriage was of indecently short duration. Well, there didn't seem to be any point in prolonging the agony. And I had stopped pining for Ralph a long time ago. Just after the crash, in fact. It frightened me. For all my geisha tendencies, I resisted being a tragic – and possibly ridiculous – figure.

And now here Louis and I were again, starting our lives over. Or trying to. Or pretending to. The trouble was, I was still waiting to find out what my life was going to be. I was waiting for a sign so as to be sure. Louis' original telephone call had seemed like a sign, but now I was having doubts.

I was in New York and the Caribbean for three whole weeks, returning to England shortly before Christmas, feeling distanced and refreshed. While I was away, Louis and my life at home had come to seem tiny, insignificant and remote, as if viewed through the wrong end of a telescope. But, when I got back to London, I found that my mother had been taken to hospital with pleurisy and pneumonia. In Chinese medicine, grief is expressed through the lungs and surely the word 'pleurisy' must have a connection to 'pleurer'. I drove to the hospital.

My mother is a tall woman, thinner than she should be, than her frame warrants, but usually robust. Propped up in bed, she looked frail and wan. Her hands were veined and trembly. She had aged a decade in the few months since my father's death, suffered a *coup de vieux*. She could not accept that he was gone, could not believe that he would have done this to her, left her this way, without warning. But he had and her bewilderment was painful to behold. When I saw her lying there, I felt a familiar blend of affection, pity, guilt and irritation, and also the tug of reality, which reminded me, with a sudden, stabbing pain, that I was not free of Louis yet.

In the Caribbean, three thousand or so miles away, my difficult, tormented, possessive, passionate, paranoid lover seemed like a distant bad dream. In London, his cramped handwriting stared up at me from a dozen envelopes, the contents of which ranged from the adoring to the jocular to the abusive. There were at least as many messages on the answering-machine. My heart sinks yet my body yearns for his touch. For I still, as the song has it, 'require love that's made of fire/ And in his arms I find I always get that kind'.

I wanted desperately to see him. The little London flat which I had just bought was in chaos. The builders hadn't yet finished and it was impossible to imagine that they ever would. It was full of dust and rubble and nothing could be put in its proper place. There were suitcases and boxes of books and china everywhere. The garden was a sea of mud. The skies were grey. My mother was seriously ill. My father was dead. This was reality.

Louis comes to see me around six. On the telephone he has been sulky and resentful, hurt that I hadn't called from overseas. He has had a fall and cut his head, just above his right eye, in the eyebrow. He fell down the stairs in the country. He tells me that Sara was 'totally unsympathetic'; she said he had only himself to blame for the accident: he was drunk. I can see her point. But I am moved to pity. Oh, Louis, my wild child, my poor, sad baby, what am I to do with you? A lethal fusion of the maternal and the sexual binds me to him. When I tell him how I feel, he looks repelled and says coldly, 'Well, there's nothing filial in my feelings for you.' But surely he doesn't really think that he is a grown-up.

Now I take him in my arms – his cheeks are rosy with cold; it's freezing outside – and I reassure him that he is as handsome as ever (the potential damage to his looks is what is worrying him). It's true. The cut – which will leave him with a raised scar that I cannot really see but can feel with my fingertips if I run them along his eyebrow – manages to make him look rather rakish.

'You're very brown,' he says suspiciously, tugging my sweater over my head. He is convinced that I have been unfaithful to him (as indeed I have). He equates a suntan with betrayal and makes as much fuss as he feels fits the occasion. I think it's as much for form's sake as anything else. What he really minds is that I went away and deserted him. He, of course, has been leading his 'normal' life with Sara. Knowing Louis as I do, this will not have included abstinence. Does that count as being unfaithful to me? Or is infidelity, as I suspect, a one-way street? A married man (and Louis might as well be married) cannot be unfaithful to his mistress with his wife.

Louis has brought me a big bunch of Stargazer lilies and a bottle of pink champagne. With difficulty, I search through my jumbled possessions to find a vase for the flowers and two glasses. Then we go to bed. I have just put clean sheets on the bed but, within seconds, they too are covered with a film of dust; I feel the fine grit beneath my shoulders as I welcome Louis back into my body.

He enters me and I know that I have not been

unfaithful, merely expedient. As he touches me, I can feel myself becoming whole once more. We complete each other. I once was blind and now can see.

For a time. A couple of days. A week at most.

Louis and Sara are taking a little holiday after Christmas. *Now* he tells me. It has been planned for months, he swears, long before he and I even . . . I wonder if this is true or if it's revenge for my going to the Caribbean. In the event, what can I do? I don't much like it but I will accept it, as I do everything. Shrinks have a phrase for it: the familiarity of abuse. Sara has, of course, made all the arrangements.

As a result of their imminent departure, she is busy, busy, busy in the run-up both to Christmas Day and to the day they leave. Louis is free to spend time with me. We are together every spare moment. I write in my diary:

> I've been seeing Louis – seeing and sleeping with. He's completely mad – much madder than I realized. On lithium every day to keep the manic depression at bay. Drinking like a fish. Fucking like a dream. Says he loves me, that I'm the only reason that he doesn't want to die.

He is convinced – I don't know why – that he will die before he is sixty. Sometimes, in the morning, I hear him talking to himself as he stares in the bathroom mirror. He says, 'I'm still here. I'm not dead yet.'

On Christmas Eve, around tea-time, I go to my brother's house; there the whole family (what's left of it) has gathered to exchange presents. I leave around seven and rush straight to Louis' apartment where we spend the rest of Christmas Eve and Christmas night together in bed. In the morning, he gives me my present. It is a diamante bracelet: very pretty, very glittery and very, very fragile. It's like our relationship. It can't survive. It isn't strong enough. None the less I put it round my wrist where it sparkles like real diamonds. By the afternoon, one of the stones has dropped out. I spend hours looking for the missing stone, fail to find it and eventually take the bracelet to a man in Soho who replaces the stone, warning me that the piece of jewellery is really for show, not for wear.

I give Louis a beautiful, yellow bowl from Morocco (it's a 'good' yellow, but when I next look for it, it is at the back of a kitchen cupboard, better hidden even than his wedding photographs, which he also keeps in a kitchen cupboard under the sink – and chipped). As an extra present, I give him a CD of the Number One Christmas hit, Mariah Carey's boppy 'All I want for Christmas is You'. Louis puts it on the player and starts dancing. Damn. (Louis is a terrible dancer.) It's dance music all right but that's not why I bought it. I bought it for its sentimental lyrics.

Louis and Sara fly off to Madrid at dawn on Boxing Day and are away for barely one week. I spend the time putting the flat in order – the builders have finished – and getting to know my new neighbourhood. (By a coincidence too bizarre to be coincidence, I have come to live in a square that backs on to the mews where I lost my virginity. I walk past Damon's old house; there is a sky-blue Karmann Ghia parked outside.)

My new home is small but perfect. It has wooden

floors, an open fireplace and no doors. I have a garden at the back and another one in the front; at present the front garden is nothing but bare earth. I shall plant roses and peonies. I shall be very happy here. With Louis gone, I am able to make plans, plans for a tidy future. With Louis out of the way, I can rest. I can create order out of disorder, realizing, as I do so, that I am simply waiting for Louis to come back and once again cause chaos. I miss him.

I knew, almost to the minute, the time of their return and I waited for Louis to call me. He didn't – not for six days. And when he did, he was drunk and perfectly vile. He had not had a good holiday. Sara had spent the week threatening to leave him if he didn't break with me once and for all. He swore to her that he had but she wouldn't believe him. She was right not to, of course; he was lying all along and she knew it. She had read his diary. She knew he had been seeing me and she knew he was lying to her.

Poor Sara, the spectator – and the spectre – at our wedding feast, watching anxiously on the sidelines; waiting, I suppose, I guess, for Louis to come to his senses, just as a wife might wait for a husband to get over a mad, mid-life infatuation. I don't know what Louis told her. As little as possible, I imagine. I only know what Louis told me he told her and Louis was a liar. Drunks always are. They have to be, as do philanderers, and that was what Louis was – a drunk and a philanderer. But what a charming, handsome, brilliant, sexually indefatigable drunk and philanderer. Which presumably was why Sara and I both loved him so and forgave him his many trespasses.

A week later he rang again, this time sweet as pie. He had found out that she'd read his diary (she had scribbled some comments in the margin – brave girl, secretly I applauded her courage). Now it was her turn in the doghouse. In bed that afternoon, he told me that he went to see Goya's 'Maja Nuda' at the Prado in Madrid and thought of me. The Maja is lush and very dark. Sara looks much more like her than I do but I accepted the compliment in the spirit that it was offered. He also told me that Sara cut short their visit to the museum because she wanted to 'drag' him off to bed. He went – willingly, I imagine.

Women often make the mistake of believing that good sex is unique to a particular pairing, that it is reciprocal, that love makes all the difference. This is both true and not true. Louis probably had just as good a time in bed with Sara as he did with me. For most men, sex is sex.

And so it continued. Sometimes I felt as if I were living in a French farce. Early one evening I drove Louis home. Sara was sitting on the doorstep, waiting for him. Louis made me drive on and stop round the corner out of sight. I barely had time to register a dark, anxious face, a tall body. Another time, Sara let herself into Louis' flat while I was in the bedroom getting dressed. I skulked upstairs, not daring to move until I heard the front door slam after them. Louis liked to cut it fine. I think it gave him an extra *frisson*, made him feel that he was a bit of a dog. Life with Sara, without me, had been safe but dull. Sara seemed not to mind about – or perhaps, after years of practice, was simply better equipped to deal with – his drinking, manic depression and the vile abuse that

tended to accompany extreme episodes. Louis was so
fragile that he clung to Sara and their 'normal' life
together as a child clings to his mother's hand. Me, he
perceived as 'exciting' but also 'dangerous'. He had
learnt, I suppose, that he shouldn't take risks.

I had yet to learn that lesson. But I did have reser-
vations about our affair. I was not at all sure that
responsibility for his well-being was a burden that I could
carry alone and his illness made me anxious. But it was
the drunkenness that I couldn't stand. Drunk, he went in
for an astonishing range of abuse and invective, but more
than his cruelty, I hated to see him diminished, silly,
childish and gabbling in baby-talk which was always a
signal that a volley of vicious insults was imminent.
Because I loved him, it was extremely painful to despise
him. He could see the contempt in my face and it made
him hate me.

Louis loved me or, at any rate, most of the time wanted
me enough to make a stab at juggling his life so as to
accommodate me and the demands that my presence in
his life made. However, the practical and emotional
difficulties created by the mere existence of the
relationship rendered Louis first anxious and desperate,
then angry. He took that anger out on me.

He knew how to hurt and humiliate me, to make me
feel small and worthless. At such times I would think,
'Sara's welcome to him.' He had no scruples about saying
the unsayable. Sometimes it was so extreme as to be
almost funny. Late one night, he telephoned to say that
he had just been in the garden and seen 'a slug with your
face on it'. He would call five or six times in a row, not
making sense, just shouting abuse – the same old words

'fat', 'ugly', 'stupid', 'boring'. The diatribe left me un-moved. I couldn't take it seriously. Once, when finally I had stopped answering and switched on the machine, he left a message saying, 'If you don't answer, I'll telephone you to death.' That made me laugh and, of course, I forgave him.

And, within hours, he'd forget whatever it was that he had said and so would I. His madness (I hate to use that word, but it's the right one) gave him an edge, made him more vivid than other people. His cruelty was balanced by sudden bursts of tenderness – he would hold my hand as we walked and suddenly stop to kiss me under a street-lamp. And his smile made my heart turn over; in repose, his face looked tortured and unhappy, but when he smiled, his expression was almost unbearably sweet.

I, too, had a talent, it seemed, for remembering only the good times. It came in handy now and enabled me to forget everything that was wrong between us. I lost count of our make-ups and break-ups. Ten days on, three weeks off, month after month. I couldn't take them, Louis, any of it, seriously, yet it hurt in a strange, distanced sort of way. Only sex felt real: lying together, closely embraced, limb upon limb, was the only time that Louis and I engaged in any way that seemed relevant.

All the 'What *shall* we do? What *can* we do? Our love is *doomed*' conversations seemed absurd. I wonder now to what extreme degree Louis' daily cocktail of drink and drugs fogged his perception. In one conversation about the impossibility of it all, I asked him, 'Do you mind about this at all?' He answered, sounding utterly wretched, 'Yes, I mind so much that I can't bear to talk about it for another minute.' And I thought, 'Yes, he does care,' but simultaneously I remembered that manic depressives live in the here and now. At that moment, I am sure he did mind desperately.

But for most of the time, the whole thing seemed, as John had said all those years ago, like 'one big movie'; yet I felt like an invalid. I had a constant nagging pain – heartache, a sense of loss and betrayal – which coloured everything. I couldn't let go. The relationship had developed a life, a momentum of its own, which was quite separate from the individuals involved in it. It was as if Louis, Sara and I were actors in a drama from which we couldn't escape; mechanically, we ran through our lines over and over again. I hated the feeling of powerlessness; it was overwhelming and frightening. I would say to myself, 'You must stop this, break free of it. It's dragging you down,' but I couldn't. I understood now why couples stayed in bad marriages for years. It was fear, not of being alone, because there is no loneliness so great as the kind you experience in an unhappy relationship, but of being without the relationship, even of being without the unhappiness.

This was the worst time of all. The winter dragged on. Grey day succeeded grey day. The skies were opaque and drained of colour; night came early. I woke in the dark and went to bed in the dark. The peculiar gloom of the English winter echoed the drabness of my life. I worried about money. In the weeks and months immediately following my father's death, I had been enveloped in the excitement of my love affair with Louis. Now that excitement had gone. In its place, there was only an ache.

Seventeen

In one of the longer 'off' periods, a girlfriend who lived round the corner from my new flat persuaded me to come out one evening with her, her Zairean boyfriend and a friend of his. We went to Covent Garden to hear a West African band. It was nice to be out, nice to flirt, to listen to music and to dance, especially with someone who could stay upright, let alone move to the music with grace and elegance.

With Louis, a whole host of things were simply not possible: dancing was only one of them. Actually, music, as a whole, was a kind of dead zone, though, like most people who are not musical, he was unaware of any lack of sensitivity in this direction. His taste in music was horrible – late at night, when he was drunk, he would turn the volume up high on his stereo and play Leonard Cohen over and over again, tunelessly singing along to 'Like a bird on a wire/ I have tried all my life to be free'. Sometimes, when his moods were less black, he would play old Supremes and Dusty Springfield singles and want to dance with me. He danced like almost every other Englishman I have ever met – stiffly, jerkily, woodenly, without any feeling for the music or for his own body. Like a puppet on a string. Or somebody suffering from St Vitus' dance. Or Tourette's Syndrome. Or both.

There is a theory that if a man is a good lover, he is a good dancer. Louis was proof of the fallacy of this hypothesis. When he wanted to dance, he was usually almost too drunk to stand and 'dancing' would consist of swaying on the spot, listening to something in his head while I tried to ensure that he didn't fall over and crash into the furniture. He once told me that he and his wife had won a dancing competition in Corsica. What kind of dancing, I wondered? Morris dancing? Clog dancing?

Fabrice, however, was a wonderful dancer. Zaireans dance in a formal and distant fashion, as if the dancers are performing a kind of present-day minuet, but its intricate patterns are underlaid with an intrinsic sensuality and understanding of how the body works.

After our night out, Fabrice took to calling me. It was an almost old-fashioned courtship: he would telephone, often twice a day, apparently for no other reason than to inquire after my well-being. His behaviour was formal, like his dancing – which was absurd, really, given that what he wanted was to sleep with me.

At first I was glad of the attention, then I became impatient. Finally, one day after he had asked yet again, with exquisite courtesy, whether it might be possible some time for us to meet, I agreed and suggested that he come the following evening for a drink. My girlfriend thought it would be good for me to see someone else. I thought she might be right. I hadn't heard from Louis for nearly four weeks.

Fabrice was punctual and strikingly dressed in a full-length black leather coat, leopardskin cap and leather trousers. Zaireans are great dressers. He came in and we sat down to drink white wine and make polite conversation. But there was nothing much to say, so when, after twenty minutes, he put his arm around my shoulders and moved to kiss me, I made no objection. I felt a stoical inevitability.

Under his leather Fabrice wore a fine, white woollen vest and long underpants. They looked old-fashioned but were almost certainly not; probably they were the creation of some up-to-the-minute designer, Jean-Paul Gaultier or Yohji Yamamoto perhaps. He began to make efficient love to me; he knew all the moves. I knew them too. *'As-tu joui?'* he asked politely. Did you come? 'Yes, yes,' I said. I lied. Once *he* had come, I couldn't wait for him to leave. This was the measure of my desperation, that I would sleep with a man for whom I didn't care, didn't even fancy, in the hope that it would make me feel better.

Fabrice telephoned every day for about a week after that night, hoping to be invited back for a repeat performance. No invitation was forthcoming. It wasn't his fault but he hadn't made me feel better. If anything, I felt worse. My one-night stand with Fabrice reminded me of the boys with whom I had slept when I was young and how I had felt then: ashamed and confused. Now there was an added exasperated weariness. I should have known better. It's ridiculous. I have done – I should perhaps say I have 'had' – so many one-night stands; but they don't suit me. I'm told the Australians have a term for it: 'sport fucking'. Well, it's not for me and you would think that I would know it by now. I want love: to love and to be loved. But I don't learn.

Finally Fabrice asked my girlfriend why I didn't want to see him. He boasted, puzzled, 'I made her come more than once, you know.' (Men really can't tell; they also seem not to have learnt that women fake it *and* lie.) Even if that had been true, it wouldn't have made any difference. She told him that I had gone back to my old boyfriend. By then, that was true.

At the beginning of April, just as it looked as if the winter might finally be coming to an end, I went abroad for six weeks. This sojourn had been planned for months – since the previous summer, before my father's death. Now it was more necessary than ever.

Travel has always been a kind of solution for me; a friend once accused me of being 'addicted to travel' and when I told Louis, with whom I was back on terms (the usual ones, no better), that I was going abroad again, he said bitterly: 'But of course you won't be here. You always just go away.' It's true. Going away separates me from my problems, but it also enables me to solve them; it gives me the necessary perspective.

This time I went to a ravishing, cold house on a Greek island, Naxos, Ariadne's island, the largest and most fertile of the Cyclades, where I read and wrote and slept and dreamed. The first night I dreamed about my father. I had a dream that I had dreamt before, that my mother had sent my father away to die on his own. I woke for an hour around four a.m. – I could see the full moon from my bed, which faced the window, and hear the steady rush of the sea – and then I fell asleep again and dreamt that I went to my father's funeral and that he was there too. I had had this dream, too, earlier, just days after my father died.

The house, which belonged to an old American woman

who lived in New Orleans and went there for only two weeks every year, was at the very top of the island, in the old, fortified *castro* built by the Venetians, and had once been the residence of the former governor of the island. It dated back to the thirteenth century and had a glorious *salone*, white, two storeys high, with a timbered ceiling. I loved that house. It was quiet as a sepulchre and as beautiful as anything I had ever seen. It refreshed the spirit and cleared the mind. After a week there, I felt as cleansed as if I had been baptized in the river of Jordan into the one, true faith. As the weeks went by, it grew warmer and it was hard not to respond to the siren call of the countryside just bursting into spring; the fields were full of wild flowers and the sound of birds and insects coming to life again. With spring came optimism.

Louis, of course, had interpreted my absence as desertion but, once I was no longer around, he began to miss me frantically and telephoned me at all hours of the day and night – sometimes sober, sometimes drunk, rarely abusive, often loving. And, physically removed from him, safe, I fell in love all over again. I asked him, 'What will our future be?' He said, 'We'll have a very long affair – for a hundred or so years – and make each other very happy.' He wrote to me too, a letter in which he said, 'I've been thinking about you a great deal lately, and I can now hold my hand out straight as a dye (if shaking slightly), and say you are my one and only.'

A Greek island out of season has a peculiar loneliness to it: it draws in on itself, it seems to repel strangers and develops a closed, introverted quality quite different from that of the warm, summer nights when tourists and islanders alike stroll along the *paralia*, the seafront, until the early hours. Fishing and tourism (and, in some cases, a modicum of agriculture) are the mainstays of the islands and these pursuits have to go into hibernation in the winter months. To my surprise, I found that I preferred the island like this – in slow mode. It was as if I had suddenly been accepted into a secret society, or had been permitted an intimacy not usually vouchsafed to strangers.

I loved my life on the island. It seemed so simple. In the mornings, I would work; at lunch-time, eat some bread and cheese and a big, messy tomato and drink some wine; in the afternoons, I would read and then, looking out at the square of blue sky that was all I could see from my bedroom window, fall into a deep sleep; I would wake around four or five and work again for a few hours. Around ten, when the wind was up and whistling through the narrow alleyways of the *castro*, I would walk down in the dark to the cheap *souvlaki* restaurant near the port and eat a *souvlaki* in pitta bread and drink a small jug of home-made *retsina*, which was so coarse it could have doubled as paint-stripper.

I had brought an old Greek grammar with me which had belonged to my father and which I would take to dinner with me. My father had marked certain, some-times unexpected, words in the grammar: the words for 'joy', 'girl', 'bottle', 'ready' and 'wonderful' all had a red asterisk next to them, as did such phrases as των ψυχων meaning '(All) souls' (day)' and δεν πειραζει ('it doesn't matter'). He had scribbled sample sentences in his big, illegible handwriting (which only those who knew him well could decipher): μου αρεσει να κολυμπω με το φεγγαρι, which means 'I like bathing by moonlight'; 'Give me a bottle' and 'She is a beautiful girl'. It gave me a strange frisson to read these words and phrases, as if my father were sending me messages from the grave.

Every night I would memorize – or try to memorize – a couple of new words and practise on the old fishermen who were always there, smoking, drinking and watching television. I was almost always the only woman, but I didn't mind and nor, it seemed, did they. If I missed an evening at the *souvlaki* place, the following night the old boys would ask me where I had been and if I was all right. How was my work progressing, they inquired politely. I had learnt the Greek for work, δουλεια, and book, βιβλιο; also γραφω, meaning 'I write'. 'It's going fine,' I would tell them, and they would smile contentedly, like proud parents, and offer me another glass of wine.

On Sunday mornings at nine thirty I went to mass in the tiny Roman Catholic cathedral, which stood directly across the little *piazza*, opposite my front door. I could just manage to follow the sung mass which was conducted in a mixture of Latin (which I remembered from school) and Greek. The priest was a middle-aged Jesuit with a neat beard and moustache. He came from the island but had spent years in Rome before coming home to take charge of the parish. His head bobbed tremulously throughout the service as if he was suffering from Parkinson's disease but he had a beautiful baritone voice and when he sang his tremors vanished.

I loved the domed, white marble cathedral – outside so light and bright, inside so dark, like an ancient Orthodox church or a cellar – with its icons of the Archangel Michael; of St Charles Borromeo, the sixteenth-century reformer, and of the Virgin Mary surrounded by stars. My favourite icon depicted St Rock, the pilgrim and healer, silver-topped staff in hand, standing in a haunting, moonlit landscape, his hunting dog hard on the heels of his silver boots. During these services, which never lasted more than an hour, I felt always a sense of peace and a deep, solemn tearfulness, as if simultaneously nothing could touch me and everything that was important was contained within these walls.

One Saturday morning there was a wedding in the cathedral. The bride, a chunky girl with a bright, eager face, wore a short dress, which surprised me. It was white, to be sure, and her hair was covered by a short veil but the dress showed her knees. The men all wore dark suits and children, dressed like miniature adults, ran about throwing handfuls of confetti. In the cobbled square outside my house, the honeysuckle was already flowering and scenting the air.

Louis and I made a plan to meet, at the end of my six weeks, in Istanbul. I wanted to revisit the island of Buyukada, the largest of the Princes' Islands in the Sea of Marmara; Louis wanted to go to Troy. In Buyukada there is, or was, an old wooden hotel where I had always wanted to stay. Louis rang and spoke to the receptionist – he spoke some Turkish – to book a room, then, very pleased with himself, he rang me and told me that the room was only $20 a night. We were to go for a week. I was intensely ambivalent about the trip: part of me looked forward to it, part of me worried. A whole week – who knew what might happen? Then, the night before I was due to fly to Turkey, he telephoned me in Athens to say that he had cracked a couple of ribs and couldn't travel. I had no way of knowing if this was true or not. I couldn't change my flight and, rather than go to Istanbul alone, stayed on in Athens.

This was one of the many small tragedies which, in retrospect, seem like the sum of my affair with Louis: we tried so hard. We made so many plans. All doomed to failure. But nevertheless, at the news that we weren't going to spend that week in Istanbul, I felt only relief.

Eighteen

Louis did eventually break up with Sara, a couple of weeks after I returned from Greece. The final rupture took the form of what must have been a horrendous scene that lasted almost an entire night. It had begun when Sara rang his doorbell while he was talking to me on the phone. He was enjoying the conversation so much that he didn't go to the door. Eventually she let herself in with her own key, to discover him lying on the sofa talking to me. I don't remember what he was saying but, whatever it was, it didn't please her. Louis laid the receiver down and, at my end, I could just make out faint, reproachful tones. Then the line went dead, although the argument continued. Sara walked out in tears, only to resume the row by phone after she arrived in her own home. When Louis woke up in the morning, after only a few hours' sleep, he found thirteen messages, each one more hysterical than its predecessor, on his answering-machine. He fled to the little house that they shared in the country and took the phone off the hook. Then, on Sunday, he drove to see me at my mother's house to tell me the good news, that he was mine, all mine.

He arrived around noon. My mother and I were in my father's study, sorting through his possessions. The day was warm, rather than seriously hot, but Louis' face was clammy and his hands were shaking so badly that at lunch he could barely hold a knife and fork.

When I went into the kitchen to get some plates, my mother, standing at the stove, asked, 'Darling, what's the matter with him? Does he have Parkinson's?'

'No,' I said, 'just a hangover.'

But he was on his best behaviour, only one glass of white wine, and all the charm he could muster.

When we left to drive back to London, my mother squeezed my arm as she kissed me goodbye and whispered, 'He's so handsome.' It was true: no excess could mar the perfection of his beauty.

That night, as we composed ourselves for sleep, preparing ourselves for our new life together, Louis said, 'Don't take this amiss, but you know, darling, it wasn't you I was in love with all those years ago. It was your father.'

I didn't take it amiss. To tell the truth, I was flattered.

But I was wrong to be. Louis was still, if not actually in love with my father, in love with his memory and with the extension of my father that he – quite wrongly – perceived me to be. And I was so filled with grief and confusion that I thought that Louis being in love with my father was perfectly right and proper. Certainly better than being in love with me.

My father's death had shaken me profoundly. I could no longer take anything for granted, and so I forgot the lessons that I had learnt over the years. I was thrown into chaos; I felt that I was at a crossroads, stranded and unsure how to proceed. Part of the trouble was that I was still waiting to find out what my life was going to be, still waiting to be sure, aware only that the things which I had expected from it had not so far materialized.

What were these things I expected? Some of them were concrete: a husband, a house, a child, maybe two. When I was a little girl, grown-ups were forever asking me what I wanted to be when I grew up. I envied those children who could say, with absolute certainty: a nurse; a ballerina; a vet. I didn't know. Nothing was clear. I thought I wanted to write, but write what? I wanted to be successful, though I doubted that would make me happy. I wanted to be happy but I didn't know what would make me happy.

At the end of the street where I live in London there used to be a cluttered, dark, little restaurant called La Bougie. A candle in a wine bottle had been placed on each table. The candles must have been replaced every so often, but somehow they always seemed to be half-burnt down, the bottles overflowing with creamy wax that had been allowed to accumulate in a mass until it spilled on to the wooden tables. The piles of wax were irresistible; you couldn't stop yourself from picking at them, playing with them. The walls were dark brown, streaked black in parts from the guttering flames of the candles and a thousand cigarettes.

La Bougie's menu comprised old-fashioned, rather heavy French food: soapy, grey *rillettes; foie de veau*; vast, bloody *entrecôtes à la bordelaise*; chicken cooked with cream, lemon and tarragon. I liked this kind of food. It was the sort of food that I liked to cook, as well as eat. The restaurant also had a serious wine list.

Its proprietor, Eric, had the sad face of a heavy drinker with a history of failed love affairs. He appeared to run the restaurant for his own amusement, rather than as a commercial venture. He and Louis got on well, presumably sensing some depressed and depressing kinship. He would sometimes sit himself heavily down at our table and talk to us, helping himself to a glass of wine from our bottle. The service was always slow. There was only one waitress; I think Eric did the cooking. I often wondered how he kept the restaurant going. It had been there for years, it wasn't expensive and there were rarely any other customers. That was one of the reasons I liked it.

The other was that Louis' drinking and the unpredictable nature of his moods made going to restaurants something of a ordeal. The part of town where he lived was a minefield, full of bars and restaurants from which he had been ejected. He would only tell me that there had been trouble in a place once we were already seated and looking at the menu. 'The last time I came here,' he would announce carelessly with a smile that combined ruefulness and pride, 'I was asked to leave.' Dinner would pass in a fog of nerves and embarrassment while I waited for something terrible to happen, for the manager to recognize him and ask us to go. As a result I was always overly polite, fawning to the waiter in the hope of appeasing him in advance. Often, by the time the bill came, Louis was too drunk to fill in the credit-card slip and I would do it, leaving a large, pacifying tip.

In La Bougie, either nobody cared or there was nobody to care. It was here that Louis first raised the subject of children.

He wanted a child; he wanted me to have his child. A boy for preference.

'It'll be a boy,' he said, 'called Henry.'
'Not Henry,' I said.

The question of children only added to my confusion. For many years I thought that having a baby would make me happy. That I didn't have one, hadn't had one, made me unhappy.

I have, in fact, been pregnant four times. The first pregnancy, like the others, was the result of carelessness. It happened when I was twenty-seven. One damp afternoon I had gone for a walk in Richmond Park with my boyfriend and left my bag in the car in full view on the seat. Somebody smashed the window and took it. I was so upset that when we got back home and fell into bed, I forgot to put in my cap. Shrinks claim not to believe in accidents – so perhaps I was trying, if not actually to replace my lost bag with a baby, at least to compensate for my loss.

There didn't seem to be any question of my having the baby. Mark, the baby's father, my boyfriend at the time, didn't love me. He loved – or thought he loved – a troublesome, dark-haired Maltese woman (she got pregnant around the same time and dealt with it in the same way as I did).

To be fair to him, I don't think I loved him either, except in the way you love someone for whom you have a brief, inexplicable, insatiable, sexual passion. So I had an abortion. Doctors prefer to say 'termination' (which the dictionary interprets as 'the end of something in time or space'), even though, or perhaps because, it sounds so cold. An abortion is defined first as 'the spontaneous or induced expulsion from the womb of a nonviable human foetus', and second as 'the failure of a project or attempt' – which, in the context of a child, has an obvious poignancy. An abortion *is* just what it sounds like: something which has gone wrong.

Mark drove me to the clinic: it was in a massive, shabby, vaguely Art Deco building, tiled so that it resembled a public lavatory and located somewhere in the no-man's land north of Oxford Street. Taped to the inner surface of the door to my room were notices in English and in Arabic; notices which spelt out rules and regulations ('No Smoking', instructions as to how to summon nurses and check-out times, like you get in a cheap hotel). Crudely carved into the pale wood of my bedside table, presumably by a previous patient who had possessed a penknife, were emphatic Spanish words. Mark had offered to pay for the operation (which cost £215), but I wouldn't let him – even though he was rich and I was not. I reasoned, confusedly, that, as he didn't love me or want the baby, it would be humiliating to let him pay (the irony was, of course, that if he had loved me and wanted the baby, perhaps no one would have had to pay for an abortion).

Mark had brought me a book to read while I was in the clinic. This was Lisa St Aubin de Terán's *The Slow Train to Milan*, the story of a beautiful, eccentric girl who falls in with some South Americans, marries one of them, though she is barely seventeen, then goes on to lead a romantic, bohemian life, much of it in Italy. The novel, which seemed to mirror much of the writer's own life, made me feel a little envious and sad.

As requested, I put on a white paper hat and white paper gown which tied at the neck and hung open at the back (there were plastic bags like shower caps for my feet), then lay, reading *The Slow Train to Milan*, on my hard, single hospital bed, waiting for my turn for anaesthetic and operation. When two nurses came to take me down to the operating theatre, I began to cry. The nurses, one on either side of me, patted my hands briskly, saying, 'There, there, it'll be all right.' Clearly, they were used to this.

When I came round from the anaesthetic, I was in so much pain that I concentrated on screaming and forgot to be depressed about the loss of my baby. A week later, at the Albert Hall to hear Van Morrison, I realized that the girl sitting directly in front of me had been the occupant of the room next to mine at the clinic.

The next time I became pregnant, I was in my early thirties – the dangerous time. (A flamboyant Italian photographer, Kenyan via Rome, once told me, 'If you can manage to get through your early thirties – *questo periodo pericoloso* – without having children, you'll be fine.' She herself had given birth to two daughters at that time in her life and subsequently cursed them as millstones, curbing her freedom.)

There was clearly some truth in the Italian woman's words; suddenly my body seemed to cry out to conceive and (again unintentionally) I was pregnant. This time I did get married, though I lost the baby after three months, some time before the wedding. My third and fourth (last) pregnancies followed the same pattern. (The third pregnancy was bound to fail because it was ectopic – occurring inside the fallopian tube.) With both miscarriages the baby quietly died inside me after about twelve weeks in the womb. I never had a proper miscarriage – blood and cramps – but each time my body would suddenly feel different, and that would be because the baby had died. This kind of miscarriage is known as a 'lost' abortion.

Around the time of the second miscarriage, I happened to read a poem by Derek Walcott. Called 'Endings', it seemed to encapsulate all that I felt. 'Things do not explode,/ they fail, they fade . . .' A friend in New York took a handkerchief of mine to a psychic, who said, 'Your friend is pregnant. She really wants this baby but her body isn't going to let her.'

It became increasingly difficult for me to believe that I was destined to be a mother, though this didn't stop me from bursting into tears whenever I saw a new-born baby on television, in the cinema or even in real life. But as each pregnancy failed, I eventually more or less ceased to believe in the idea of myself as a mother. Also I began to feel too old – even if, clinically, I wasn't. Motherhood, at least for the first time, I thought, was for the young.

Louis didn't know about any of this; what amounted to a hugely significant part of my past. While we were together, I felt unable to mention (let alone explain) my erratic periods and my irregular bleeding (in what may have been a physical response to the loss of my father, I had begun to bleed on the day of his funeral). He knew nothing about my miscarriages nor about my doubts as to my suitability as a mother, and I couldn't tell him.

Actually, I couldn't really tell him anything much. Partly, I couldn't talk to him because I didn't trust him: I didn't trust him not to throw my confidences back in my face later. Partly I couldn't talk to him because he didn't want to listen, and partly he simply didn't understand me. We didn't speak the same language. Louis, like many men, liked to talk about subjects, tangible subjects which interested him: history, poetry, gardening, Russian literature. But he wasn't much good at conversation. Louis' notion of conversation was simply for him to impart information and for me to listen open-mouthed. Because he really did know so much, it was some time before I got over being impressed by his erudition, and realized that we were barely communicating.

So, even if he were sober enough to hear me, the prospect of telling him the unwelcome news that I might not be able to have his baby was just too daunting.

And he so wanted me to have a baby, his baby, and he so wanted it to be called Henry. But I hated the name 'Henry'. There was no way I would have a Henry (or, if I had anything to do with it, even a boy – my phantom child was a dear little girl called Rose whom I planned to dress in faded flower prints like an Edwardian or Pre-Raphaelite child), but I found collusion in the fantasy of Louis' and my child oddly soothing. It was somehow easier than the idea of marrying him or even just living with him. A successful marriage, someone said, is a successful meshing of neuroses and ours wouldn't have stood a chance.

But there was something sexy about the idea of 'making a baby'.

For what seemed like ages, marriage and children went together in my mind. People, I thought, married because they wanted to have or because they were going to have children. Then they had children, then they became a family. But I knew, unhesitatingly, that it wasn't for me;

I was the little match girl, my face pressed up against the window, looking in at the rosy-cheeked children gathered round the Christmas tree, and I knew that I didn't belong in a family, or not in a proper family.

Knowledge, however, didn't prevent the allure of fantasy. Louis and I and a baby. Happy Families. The truth, though, was clearly bleaker. We were lost souls, babes in the wood, clinging to each other for warmth and comfort.

But then Louis came up with the idea of Henry. And, once Louis had decided that I was going to have a baby, that we were going to be a real family, he seemed to think that that was all there was to it. But after several months had elapsed and I still wasn't pregnant, he made me go to hospital for tests. Nothing was wrong, or not anything that the doctors could see. By then, though, I suspected that this idea, indeed our whole relationship, was an illusion. There was no way we were going to live happily ever after.

In late August we decided to go to Venice for a long weekend. The choice of Venice, crowded, expensive, exquisitely beautiful and redolent of the past, was, of course, symbolic. On our first evening, once again, everything seemed possible. The sun sank into the Grand Canal, we sipped Bellinis at a pavement café and the years slipped away. We made believe, just for a moment or two, that we were very young again and had just taken the bus into Venice from my parents' house. It didn't matter that now it was high summer instead of icy January, nor that we were both twenty-six years older. It didn't matter that I no longer had *parents*, merely a mother. We could still pretend.

The juke-box was playing Gloria Estefan singing 'Con Los Años Que Me Quedan', which means 'With The Years That I Have Left', a sad and beautiful song. I had listened to it again and again at home because the song seemed almost to be about us. I didn't speak Spanish, but I could still understand.

'Listen,' I said to Louis, 'Listen to the words of the song.' Louis, who spoke perfect Spanish, listened for few moments, then turned to me and translated them.

> I know that I still have a chance
> I know it's not too late to make it up to you
> I know our love is real
> And with the years that I have left to live
> I will show you how much I love you

He leant across the table and kissed me on the mouth, closing his hand over mine. 'Is that really how you feel?' he asked.

'Yes,' I said.

'Prove it, then. Prove it. I've always loved you. Will you marry me?'

'Probably,' I answered.

Nineteen

On Guy Fawkes Night there was a huge fireworks display on Primrose Hill. It happened, apparently, every year but this was the first time that I had been there to see it. On the summit of the hill an enormous bonfire raged skywards. People danced around it, throwing branches, broken chairs, McDonald's burger wrappers, cigarette butts, whatever came to hand, on to the pyre; the flames were so high, it seemed as if they could easily consume three adult witches, let alone a single guy. Pedestrians and cars thronged and clogged the nearby streets. Louis and I parked some distance away, then walked towards the spectacle. The sky seemed alive with shooting stars and rockets exploding in showers of forked lightning: hot pink, electric green and brilliant diamond-white tracers burst over our heads.

Earlier that evening we had visited my friend who lived in the neighbourhood, the one with the Zairean boyfriend. Every summer, weather permitting, she assiduously cultivated marijuana plants in her tiny patio garden. By the autumn, harvest was complete, with superb results: a decent quantity of fine, subtle, mildly hallucinogenic grass. We had smoked a couple of joints with her before leaving for the bonfire, all the better to appreciate the fireworks.

'I love fireworks. They're so great. I am crazy, crazy, *crazy* about them,' Louis chanted over and over. I turned to look at him. He was wearing my father's tweed jacket. His face, illuminated, for a few seconds, by the kaleidoscopic starburst of a giant Catherine wheel, appeared pale and feverish under the party lights. He was sweating slightly, despite the cool air, and his eyes were burning and intense as if the scene before us was having a powerful effect on him.

'Are you all right?' I asked. (I knew by now I had to watch him, to watch over him.)

'Yes, of course, I am. I am just having a wonderful time. I'm in heaven. Heaven. I haven't had this much fun in years.' He threw back his head and laughed, his laughter high-pitched and tinged with hysteria. 'What are you on about? Don't you just adore the fireworks? They're so beautiful. I could watch them all night. Look at that one, like a starfish exploding. Lovely, lovely, lovely.'

We watched the fireworks until they ended, then we pushed our way through the crowds to where I had left the car. When we got back to my flat, Louis rolled another joint, lit it, then immediately rushed out into the square where a small group of diehards were still letting off some much smaller fireworks. I took off my clothes and climbed into bed, sleepy and stoned. A few minutes later, Louis returned, rolled another joint, then rushed outside again, saying, as he ran out the door, 'Come outside, sweetie. Why are you in bed? Bo-o-ring. Don't you want to see the lovely fireworks?' He didn't wait to hear my answer.

For another hour or so, Louis carried on in the same way, rushing in and out of the house, feverishly rolling and smoking. I could feel his excitement rising like mercury in a thermometer. Any minute now he would hit boiling or breaking point. Either prospect was alarming. I got out of bed and hid what was left of the grass in a tiny, wooden box on my bedside table. I had thought that grass might suit Louis better than alcohol, but I was beginning to have doubts.

When he finally came in, it was almost two in the morning and the firework parties had ended. His eyes were huge and bright, his pupils shrunk to pin-heads. He seemed hyper, unnaturally hyper even for him, quite unable to keep still.

'Where's the grass?' he asked.

'The grass?' I said vaguely, as if I didn't know what he was talking about. 'Isn't it over there? On the table? No? Well, you must have finished it.' He didn't look as if he believed me.

'Is there any whisky?' he asked.

'Come on, darling, not now,' I said. 'Come to bed. It's late'.

I had hidden the grass but I'd forgotten about the whisky. I heard Louis stumble off into the kitchen, then pour himself a drink. Whisky was the worst. If he drank wine or champagne, he was manageable, but whisky was too potent. I resigned myself to what was bound to be a long night.

Louis undressed, throwing his clothes on to the floor, then leapt into bed. He exuded a curious, almost feral, odour: excitement mingled with marijuana, gunpowder, wood-smoke and whisky. The combination seemed to have lit a strange fire in his blood. For the first time, his body felt alien. He ran a hand over my breasts but I could tell his mind was elsewhere. He said, 'I know there is some grass left. You must have hidden it. Where did you put it?'

He got up, naked, and began to search the room, opening drawers and cupboards at random, desperately. It was only a matter of time before he found the little box. And the last thing I wanted was a scene.

'Oh, look, here it is. I must have put it here, then forgotten about it.' Louis seized the box from me and began to roll another joint, then another. He was chain-smoking grass, one spliff after another in rapid succession as if they were cigarettes, until there was none left. It was amazing. Every so often the seeds exploded and burning fragments fell on to his bare chest, which he appeared not to notice.

The evening was a revelation: up to then I really hadn't grasped the extent to which his personality was addictive. Now I understood that whatever came his way – drink, drugs, even sex – he would be bound to consume, voraciously. There was nothing he could do in moderation.

Finally, around four, he fell asleep, with all the suddenness of a tropical sunset. Throughout the rest of the night, while Louis tossed and turned, ground his teeth and muttered unintelligibly, I dozed fitfully.

In the morning Louis seemed fine, apparently un-affected by the night's excesses. It was one of the peculiarities of his physiology: nine times out of ten he would bounce right back, like a vampire rejuvenated by indulgence. We sat together amicably over breakfast, drinking tea, eating boiled eggs and brown toast, swap-ping sections of the Sunday papers, just like an old, married couple. The radio played softly in the background, tuned to Radio Three. Mozart's Clarinet Quintet in A, at once measured and ecstatic, filled my sunny dining-room.

The music was suddenly interrupted by a news bulletin. A world leader, a major political figure, had been assassinated in the Middle East. We talked about it for a few minutes, about how catastrophic it seemed, then I went into the kitchen to make more tea. When I returned, Louis was crying, which surprised me. It wasn't that I didn't think that the news wasn't terrible. I did, but it hadn't affected me in such a personal way. He insisted, then and there, that we write a joint letter to the dead man's embassy expressing our regret and solidarity. I agreed, to humour him, and went into my study to type it out.

I came back with the letter in my hand and realized immediately that Louis was different. I knew it, even before he opened his mouth. He was drunk.

'You've been drinking,' I said incredulously. It was half-past nine in the morning. I had been out of the room for less than ten minutes. 'How can you be drunk? I've only been gone a minute.' I pushed past him into the kitchen. On the table, in the centre of the table, its top off, was an empty bottle of Fernet Branca, the bitter Italian herb digestive which is supposed to get rid of hangovers. It normally lay at the bottom of my wine rack and the last time I'd looked at it, it had been three-quarters full. The bottle had lain on the rack for over a year. A tiny glass of it is more than enough to do the trick as far as hangovers are concerned; no one normal would drink nearly a whole bottle. Indeed, no normal person would drink it for pleasure: it tastes like cough mixture. But Louis wasn't normal. Not now, not ever.

'Oh, for God's sake, this is really too much', I said. He stood, swaying in front of me, looking foolish and faintly rueful.

'I was upset,' he said.

'So upset that you had to drink nearly a whole bottle of Fernet Branca for breakfast? Oh, please. Give me a break.' I sat down, disheartened and furious. Louis' behaviour had cheapened his pain. I understood now why I had sensed something false about his tears.

'Sit down, please,' I said. 'Listen to me. Please. I do not want to go out with a drunk. I do not want my lover to be someone who drinks three-quarters of a bottle of Fernet Branca first thing in the morning. I don't find it funny or sexy or endearing. I find it pathetic and disgusting. Do you understand?'

Louis looked at me, not so much like a scolded child, but more like a dog which knows that it shouldn't have made a mess on the carpet or stolen some food off the table, but would do the same thing again and again — given the chance. There was no remorse in that look. Louis was too truculent to feel remorse. He never apologized for anything. And he didn't really see why his drinking was a problem. I like to drink (I hate being drunk), but I had offered to give up alcohol if it would help him. Louis didn't want that. What he wanted was to drink. He didn't care what I did. My drinking had nothing to do with his.

Most of the time he didn't even admit there was a problem. At first and for quite a long time, months actually, I believed him. I wanted to, of course. I didn't want to believe that I was in love with a hopeless, incurable alcoholic.

This was the first time I had ever called Louis a drunk to his face. In a way, it was the first time that I had admitted to myself that he was a drunk. Over the months, inevitably, we had talked about his drinking. Invariably these discussions took place late at night, when Louis was at his most eloquent. He would have had just a bit to drink, wine or champagne, not so much that he was drunk but enough to loosen his tongue. We would be lying in bed, feeling fond and at ease with one another. At such times, he was so reasonable, so persuasive. 'Dr McEwan [a doctor who had a drying-out place in north London into which Louis had sometimes been forced] says that I'm not really an alcoholic, you know,' he'd say. Indeed, mostly, he didn't seem as if he were one. He could work impressively hard, he had great powers of concentration, he made love indefatigably and he could – at times, even often – carry on a sensible conversation. He would announce that he was going to give up drinking and there seemed to be no earthly reason why he shouldn't be able to, should he choose to. But both of us forgot that it was only drink which gave him the strength to say that he was going to do without it.

When I look back, I see this episode as a defining moment in our relationship. A watershed. Afterwards things were different. There were other episodes that marked a change, a downshift, if you like, in my tolerance, my acceptance of his behaviour, my acceptance of him, but this was the first. This was the beginning of the end.

At the start of our affair, and for months afterwards, I was so besotted with Louis and my fantasy of our future together that I believed I could take it all in my stride (and by all I didn't just mean the drinking). I would even make jokes about his appetite for booze. One Saturday morning, as Louis jumped out of bed to leave for the country with Sara, he said to me, 'Do I smell of you? Will Sara notice?' 'No,' I told him, 'you smell like a pub at closing time.' It was said without malice, with tolerant affection, and we both laughed. Another time I went into an off-licence and heard myself saying to the salesman, 'My boyfriend's a drunk. Have you got any weak wine?'

Wasn't history, particularly literary history, full of famous drunks? Famously alluring drunks. Dylan Thomas, Brendan Behan, Malcolm Lowry, F. Scott Fitzgerald – drunks every one of them. And didn't Robert Lowell have a problem too? Their women managed to put up with them. Why couldn't I handle Louis' drinking? But they were writers – Louis wasn't, though perhaps he should have been. Perhaps that made a difference. But it wasn't funny any more. The Fernet Branca incident did something to me. It made me realize that Dr McEwan was wrong. Louis *was* an alcoholic. And from that moment on, though I desired him as much as ever, though I loved him, often desperately, a kind of exhausted fatalism characterized my attitude towards him and towards the relationship.

Around this time I was reading a book of popular psychology. In it there was a chapter on fantasy. 'It is a rule of fantasy that every dream must have its corresponding nightmare,' it began. Like 'the effects of alcoholic content in the blood' on my Soho postcard, the 'fantasy cycle' too had five stages: the *Anticipation* stage; the *Dream* stage; the *Frustration* stage; the *Nightmare* stage, which was the reverse of the *Dream* stage; and finally, the *Death Wish* stage, or the 'explosion into reality'.

I applied this analysis to my affair with Louis. In our case, the *Anticipation* stage had been brief and could be said to comprise the ten days between his telephone call when I was at my father's deathbed and the moment when he told me, over dinner in a Greek restaurant, that he had always loved me. The *Dream* stage encompassed the rest of that dinner when we planned a blissful future together, the night that followed, the week that followed that night, including the dinner in the Malay restaurant, our Lampedusa conversation, and the ecstatic night and day at my parents' house in the country (excluding the unpleasant episode *en route* to the church which I had so successfully erased from my memory – at least, from the part of my memory which guided me).

The *Frustration* stage covered my attempts to get Louis to leave Sara, or at least to choose between us, and the realization that his drinking was as bad as it had ever been, and actually worse than I had feared, as well as all the conversations that we had had about it and the failure of these conversations to achieve anything positive.

The *Nightmare* stage – aptly named, I thought – encompassed the period when there was just the two of us, when there was no Sara to share the load. It included the late-night Leonard Cohen sessions, the dinners in restaurants when I would be overly, almost obsequiously, polite to the waiters in the hope that they wouldn't notice Louis and remember him from previous visits, nor care how drunk he was this time, and that Louis wouldn't fly into a sudden unreasonable rage or start one of his diatribes against the human race; it included the occasion when he telephoned me around one in the morning, not long after he had left my flat: he rang to tell me that he had just punched a taxi-driver because he had taken him home the 'slow' way. There were at least a couple of other ghastly occasions which I couldn't even bear to remember.

The *Death Wish* stage had just begun.

Twenty

The end of my affair with Louis came effectively one Thursday in late November when we went to stay with his Aunt Joan in the country.

We had been leading a 'normal' life together for about six months, since Louis split up with Sara. Couple life. We had a few dinners with friends (invariably my friends) where I would watch Louis like a hawk, unable to relax, waiting for something terrible to happen – something terrible and embarrassing or terribly embarrassing. We went to the movies – three times in all: we saw a new print of Chabrol's *La Femme Infidèle* (Louis left the cinema for fifteen minutes, desperate for a cigarette); the bloodthirsty *La Reine Margot*, about the beautiful, passionate, Catholic wife of Henri of Navarre – a film which we both loved; on the third occasion, we went to an American, black comedy which was instantly forgettable. After the first ten minutes, Louis walked out and went home to bed, saying that he was hating it. I stayed but fell asleep immediately and only woke up just before the end. After that we avoided the cinema. We didn't go to concerts, or to the theatre or to the opera. We didn't even watch television.

The weekends were spent at Louis' little house in the country. There we went for long walks and made love in the afternoon. In the evenings Louis got drunk. He seemed to drink more there, maybe because he didn't have to work the next day. He would pour glass after glass, bottle after bottle, of superb, twenty-year-old claret down his throat. Soon, all his obsessions and paranoias would rise to the surface: women – how they were all lesbians and taking over the world; Byron and the bitter tragedy of his death at the age of thirty-six from fever at Missolonghi; the number of young men who died in 1916 in the Battle of the Somme. This last was a recurrent theme and I found it particularly difficult to deal with. He would always begin in the same way, asking, 'Do you know how many men died at the Somme? Do you know?'

Perhaps I should have known. But I'm not sure I cared. 'Six hundred thousand. Six hundred thousand young lives wasted.' Another gulp. 'But what do you know? What do you care?' And on it would go till the tears ran down his cheeks and I left the room. There was nothing, in the end, I could say.

Louis' house was in the largest, the oldest, and supposedly the coldest, county in southern England. One of a pair of semi-detached farm cottages which had been built in the Forties or Fifties, it had no particular charm or distinction. But its position was magnificent, if rather exposed. It was possible to hear, in the distance, the muffled thump of guns from troops out on manoeuvres on Salisbury plain. The cottages stood on the crest of a wooded hill, with a vista across the broad sweep of the downs. I liked the wildness, the generous landscape. The house itself lacked personality. Louis was both extravagant (like the landscape) and mean (like the cottage); one of the manifestations of his mean side was to spend almost nothing on the house, because it was rented. So all the original cheap fixtures and fittings remained in place: the pink moiré three-piece suite, the deal occasional tables, the pre-fabricated kitchen cupboards, which fell to pieces if you opened the doors roughly. The whole kitchen looked as if it might collapse in a strong wind. But it was Louis' castle, essential to him, to his vision of himself, so I kept my opinions to myself, though I cursed the flimsy kitchen under my breath.

A thirtyish Cityish type named Henry rented the adjoining cottage. His succession of long-legged, honey-maned, blue-jeaned girlfriends (a different one, it seemed, every weekend – Joanna, Annabel, Lucinda, Belinda, Charlotte) were polite; they behaved towards me as if I were the same age as their mother – and I probably was. On fine Sunday mornings, Henry's braying laugh penetrated the garden fence and I would catch a whiff of an exotic but familiar herb and hear the tinkle of ice on glass. If it rained, I heard the same sounds through the thin walls between the cottages; the only difference was that I couldn't smell the marijuana. Henry liked to smoke dope. And so did Louis.

Louis would often visit Henry, saying casually, 'I thought I'd just pop over to see Henry for a bit. I'll only be twenty minutes.' He would return, glassy-eyed, a couple of hours later. This was the weekend part of our 'normal' life.

I hadn't met Joan before, but I took to her and she apparently took to me. She was a jolly woman in her sixties who, everyone said, had been a great beauty when young and whose racy past had left her in frail health. On this particular occasion she had invited us to a buffet dinner in aid of her local Conservative Party organization. Under normal circumstances, Conservative Party fundraisers would have been my idea of hell but, as Louis was desperate for 'normality', which seemed sometimes to mean that we should be accepted as a couple in polite society, I agreed to go. Joan loved Louis as if he were her son and he loved her instead of his mother; he wanted her to welcome us into her house, into her life, so I agreed to the evening with every appearance of enthusiasm – as if I had been invited to La Scala or given a ticket to a Bruce Springsteen concert.

The outing began badly. At the station, Louis discovered that he had mislaid, or lost, his wallet. A couple of large vodkas (when, oh when, will drinkers learn that it *does* smell; it has a distinctive, *vodka* smell?) on the train soothed his nerves and turned his eyes glassy. But it didn't seriously begin to fall apart until we got to the Conservative Association dinner.

Joan had lead a rackety life and seemed to have a reasonable grasp of reality, so I was surprised to discover that she seemed to believe that Louis didn't drink or, rather, had stopped drinking. But that was what she believed, and when she saw him gulp down a glass of red wine, she grew visibly nervous.

A former Cabinet minister gave a speech before dinner. It was a dull speech, with pretensions to humour, but the audience apparently lapped it up, laughing loudly in all the right places. Louis was first bored, then irritated. During dinner, boredom plus irritation turned, as often happened, to anger. Louis hated, no, actually he despised, his fellow guests and he started, alternately, to sneer at them – only just *sotto voce* – and to attempt to slide his hand up my skirt to caress my inner thigh. I felt as if I was trying to control a highly strung horse which was threatening to rear or bolt. My back and shoulders ached, as if the effort I was making was physical. Joan, from her seat at a table on the other side of the room, eyed us anxiously.

As soon as coffee had been served, she came across to us and announced that we were leaving. The evening wasn't over, the marquee was full of her friends, but she had grown scared of what Louis might do. And who could predict what Louis might do? He hadn't insulted anyone yet but the night was young. He hadn't fallen over, nor had he urinated in a corner yet, but if he drank more wine, he might well do either or both of these things. I had seen it all before.

We drove, in silence, through the still, late autumn night to Joan's pretty house. A mile or so outside the village Louis asked her to stop the car. 'I'll walk the rest of the way,' he said. 'I need some air.'

'That's it,' said Joan as we drove on, 'that's finally it. In front of all my friends. How dare he? God knows what would have happened if you hadn't been there. Sara could never have handled him like that. So, anyway, that's it. I've had it with Louis. I'm not giving him another chance.'

Louis came silently through Joan's back door. He looked combative and abashed, defiant and humiliated. It was an expression I recognized. Joan kissed me and went upstairs. She barely glanced at Louis.

Louis threw himself angrily into an armchair, saying to me, 'I wasn't that bad, was I? Well, was I?'

'Not by your usual standards, you weren't,' I said, 'but by Joan's, yes, you were. As far as she knew, you had given up drinking.'

'I don't care. I don't give a fuck. Ghastly, boring, bourgeois farts – all of them. And as for the Right Honorable with his stupid, banal, pig-ignorant speech, well, I hope he rots in hell.'

I had seen Louis like this before. And I knew that, very soon, he would turn on me. But the manner of his attack – or rather its content – took me by surprise.

'It's no good between us. It never will be,' he announced in a sorrowful, rather than an angry, tone.

He was right, of course. But perversity or masochism – perhaps a combination of the two – made me ask why, even though why was obvious.

'Because, you see, darling, I don't love you.'

This was new to me – and very hurtful.

'Darling, it's not that I don't want to. I do. But I can't love you because my heart was broken when I was young, when Anna left me. I've never been able to love anyone since. I suppose I still love her.'

Anna had left Louis twenty years ago. He had had God knows how many other women in between. He was no more in love with Anna than I was with Damon or with Ralph. And even if her leaving him had in some way scarred him (just as Damon's betrayal had scarred me), it was no longer an issue. The truth was that Louis was drunk, maudlin, anxious to deflect attention from the wreck of the evening, and not above (not remotely above) shamelessly manipulating my fragile emotions. And how well he knew how to do that.

Looking back, it is hard to believe that I can have been

completely unaware of what Louis was doing – that he was taking me for a ride, playing with me. But at the time, I immediately rose to the bait and began to cry, sobbing uncontrollably. Perhaps I was tired too. Perhaps I had drunk too much. Almost certainly the stress was having its effect on me.

As soon as I began to cry, Louis cheered up. 'I'm sorry, darling, but that's the way it is. There's nothing I can do,' he said, with a grin. He was on a roll now. He made no attempt to comfort me. Somehow we got ourselves upstairs, undressed and into bed. Once there, Louis decided to up the ante.

'Do you want to know what I did last night?' he began in a conversational tone. I didn't answer. I was sobbing into the pillows. He continued regardless.

'I went to see Sara. I went to fuck Sara. I spent the night with her.'

'Why?' I asked.

'Because I wanted to. I wanted some good, uncomplicated sex. The trouble with you is you're so unsexy. You're just not sexy. Sex is so difficult with you.'

Why did I listen to him? Why did I believe him? I did, even though I knew enough about Louis' past not to fall for his absurd behaviour. For instance, I had learnt recently that when he was younger, he had once taken a schoolfriend of mine to a hotel, and signed them in as 'Mr and Mrs John Keats'; he himself had told me that he had fucked Anna one night against a statue in Kensington Gardens. He had been around and I put nothing past him. Now he meant to hurt me.

After minutes, after maybe half an hour – it seemed as though I had spent half the night listening to Louis, crying and shaking my head in denial – I climbed out of bed and dressed. 'What do you think you're doing?' said Louis.

'I'm going. I'm leaving. I'm going back to London.'

'Don't be ridiculous. You can't. How do imagine you are you going to get there?'

'I don't know. I'll hitch a lift. I'll call a taxi from a callbox.'

Of course, I didn't go. Instead, I undressed again, got back into bed and fell asleep, my eyes red and swollen with weeping.

In the morning I woke early with acute stomach cramps. My period had started in the night. I got up and went to the bathroom. When I returned to bed, Louis half-woke and turned towards me, feeling for me in the dim light like a blind man would. My stomach began to tighten and churn, the cramps mingling with a familiar sensation of dread and desire that Louis always evoked in me.

'We can't,' I said. 'I've got my period.'

Louis sighed. I slid my hand down the length of his body and reached for his penis. It was difficult to tell which was stronger, my desire or the cramps. It was difficult to distinguish between the two sensations. The pain fuelled the pleasure. The whole of my lower body seemed to be on fire; the slow flame of desire now raged. The misery of the previous night, the dreamy, drugged hangover that is the legacy of a crying jag, the hormonal upset, the sharp pains of the cramps, my burning, aching, desperate longing for Louis: all combined in one frantic, overwhelming need. I have never felt anything like it – before or since. Nothing so intense, or so demanding. It was impossible to withstand. It was also degrading.

We made love and I bled all over the white sheets in Joan's best guest-room. When it was over, the bed looked like an abattoir and Louis, his slender thighs streaked with blood, looked like a sacrificial lamb.

'What I told you last night,' he said, 'about Sara. Well, it wasn't true.'

Twenty-one

A few days later I flew to the Caribbean. Barely two months before, Hurricane Luis had swept through the islands, with winds of nearly two hundred miles an hour, leaving havoc in its wake. In Antigua, the worst of the destruction had already been concealed by new, fresh, lush vegetation. Clouds of white butterflies filled the air like confetti. Only sheets of galvanized steel and lengths of wire distorted almost beyond recognition, twisted into fantastic shapes, still lay scattered everywhere, evidence of Luis's terrible power. I lay naked under the gauze mosquito net in my hotel room and thought about Louis.

Louis, like Luis, was, it seemed to me, a force of nature and, like the hurricane, intensely destructive. He had swept into my life and turned everything around. He had the power to make everything different, to shake it all up, to rearrange it. I thought of that last evening, of what he had said, first about Anna, then about Sara. He knew how to get to me, to make me believe that black was white, to make me doubt myself as well as doubt him. I no longer knew what was true. I didn't know if he loved me or if he ever had. The feeling, the thought, that he loved me had been the thing that kept me going, that kept us together, that made everything – all the bad times, the drinking, the madness – just about bearable. If he didn't love me, there was no point. And yet his love was as worthless as the rest. It was just words. It had no substance.

One night I dreamt about the man who 'lives' on a plot of waste land at the end of my street. Actually he isn't homeless – he has a council flat in the area – but, for reasons of his own, he prefers to spend his days, can of beer in hand, standing or squatting on a patch of waste land near my front garden. He is tallish, the top of his head is completely bald, and his remaining hair – reddish-brown – streams unkempt to his shoulders, his beard straggles down the front of his shirt. He wears, whatever the weather, a lumberjack check shirt and brown cord jeans, the latter so low on his hips that they look as if at any moment they might fall to the ground. He's outside in most weather; sometimes his hair and beard run with water until they look like wet grass on a riverbed. He is always drinking the same extra-strong beer – it comes in large, blue cans – and he smokes roll-ups. He seems to have a sort of business, dealing in rusty, second-hand bicycles, which he keeps inside three rusty vans, one of which doubles as his sleeping quarters. On good days, he can seem jovial enough, passing the time of day with anyone who goes by – people out walking their dogs, mothers taking their children to school and other vagrants. He himself has a dog which he has trained to jump up round his neck, where he wears it like a moth-eaten fur stole. But on bad days he curses and mutters about 'them' being inside in his head.

In my dream, I saw his tumescent penis poking through his fly. The dream left me uncomfortable and disgusted, also aroused. It took me some time to realize that the dream was really about Louis. When I made the connection, it disturbed me more than it is possible to imagine.

On my last day I flew over to Barbuda, a small, flat island north of Antigua with a minute population, barely more than a thousand people. Hurricane Luis had reduced Codrington, Barbuda's only village, to a shanty town. It had flooded, seriously; the island's flatness made the devastation all the more visible. Many of the houses had been made of wood, and even those made of bricks or concrete had not withstood the storm. The ground was strewn with sheets of galvanize and planks, stained with salt water. On the road was a sign which read:

> Let '95 September Be A Reminder
> Not Everything Hits A Nail is HAMMER
> Not Every man with HAMMER A BUILDER
> Learn from the Past for the Future
> 'LUIS'

The next morning, a friend took me to the airport. We went to the airport bar for a beer before my flight was called and as we stood there, drinking in the languorous Caribbean heat, I said to her: 'I'm not going to see Louis any more.'

'Honey,' she said, 'that's easy for you to say when you're here, three thousand miles away.'

'No, I mean it. It's got to finish. It's killing me.'

And I did finish it.

Twenty-two

I'm writing this in Greece. I'm in the same house that I have lived in before, the one with the white walls and the high, high ceilings. I'm listening to that Nanci Griffith song again, over and over again. It echoes round the big, white room, bouncing off the walls and reverberating against the tall windows, so that the glass shivers.

> Well, I got a heart that burns with a fever
> And I got a worried and a jealous mind
> Well how can a love
> That will last forever
> Get left so far behind?
> It's a mighty mean and a dreadful sorrow
> That's crossed the evil line today
> How can you ask about tomorrow
> When we ain't got one word to say?

This place makes me think of Louis.

I saw him about three weeks ago, just before I left to come here. I hadn't seen him for almost two years. A year and eleven months, to be precise. But one day in late August, he telephoned out of the blue. He was in hospital. He had tried to kill himself. I can't remember the words he used when he told me that he had tried to kill himself. He didn't put it quite like that; he glossed over it in a languid, self-deprecating way, but I knew immediately what he meant. Suicide was always potentially part of Louis' repertoire. And, even if it wasn't actually to be suicide that finished him off, I was always subliminally prepared for the news that he was dead, that he had killed himself in an accident, a car crash, a fire, falling off a horse, drowning. There were many ways to go, especially for someone with a death wish and that degree of self-loathing.

When Louis and I first stopped seeing each other, he used to call quite often. Sometimes drunk, sometimes sober. Sometimes straight, sometimes curly. Sometimes abusive, sometimes loving. Sometimes rueful, even realistic – 'You bring out the worst in me,' he told me on one occasion. It was always my fault. Once we even made a plan to meet, to go to see the film of *A Hundred and One Dalmatians*, but he cancelled our date without an excuse, and I felt that I had had a narrow escape. I missed him – especially in bed. I couldn't imagine sex without thinking of him and that was painful, so I stopped thinking about sex.

But I dreamt about him constantly, dreams of lust and longing. In my dreams he was *never* sober and I was *always* anxious. I remembered small, hateful details of our time together: how he couldn't stand my liking cheese ('You'll turn into a cheese,' he would say. I couldn't see why it mattered); how he always bought a wine called Jacob's Creek, an inexpensive Australian Chardonnay, one bottle at a time. To this day, the sight of a bottle of Jacob's Creek makes me shiver.

Then, after I hadn't heard from him for several

months, he called to tell me that he was getting married – to a distant cousin. All the while he was talking, I could tell that he was also listening, waiting for my reaction. I didn't want him to know how shocked I was, but actually I felt as if I had been punched in the stomach. After I had hung up, I went into the kitchen, drank a big glass of neat vodka and had a brief, bitter cry. I needn't have bothered: they didn't get married; their engagement ended when she called the police after a fight. But that evening I put away the photograph of him that I kept on my desk, a photograph I had taken one happy day when we'd been out walking in the sunshine. In it, Louis stands posed, laughing in front of an oak tree, blowing me kisses. I remember that as I pressed the shutter I said to him, 'This is for me to remember you by when we fall out.' It was my proof – proof that we had been happy.

But his letters and cards, bound together by a rubber band, remained in the drawer of my desk. There weren't many of them and I never reread them, but I knew that they were there.

For almost a year, there was silence. I nearly worried, certainly I was curious, so I asked a friend who knew a man who knew Louis whether he had heard anything. He had.

I remember the occasion clearly. I was lying in the bath at about seven in the evening and talking on the telephone, which is what I love to do: four of my favourite pleasures – a hot bath, a glass of wine, music playing, the telephone – combined into one big pleasure.

'I've been thinking about Louis,' I said. 'I suppose I would have heard if anything had happened to him, if, for instance, he was dead.'

'Well,' said my friend, 'actually, something did happen, but you're to promise, you're to swear not to tell anyone.'

'OK, I promise.'

'He was involved in this terrible car crash. He was blind-drunk, way over the limit. The car was a write-off.'

'Was he hurt?' I asked.

'No, amazingly.'

The crash had occurred some months before in the country near where he rented his little house.

In my day Louis never drove drunk. He was terrified of having an accident, or even just losing his driving licence. The cottage was remote – the nearest town and station were over fifteen miles away – and his country life, which was important to him, wouldn't be feasible without a car.

'After the crash and the court hearing,' my friend continued, 'he booked himself into a detox place in the north of England. There's a doctor there he likes. And of course he's lost his licence now.'

Poor Louis. He hadn't just lost his licence; he'd lost part of his life, the part which I'd always thought kept him, if not exactly sane, at least alive, or at any rate made his life worth living.

But months had elapsed between the crash and his call. What had happened?

This is what Louis told me when he eventually telephoned. He said that he had gone to a hotel in Rye with a woman for the weekend. On Saturday evening, before dinner, they had made love. Lying in each other's arms in the warm afterglow of good sex (a job well done, mission accomplished), she had asked for a glass of champagne. As Louis picked up the receiver to call room service, he thought, so he told me, why not make it two glasses? He swore that, before that evening, he hadn't had a drink in months. (My friend had told me that it had been one of the conditions imposed by the court after the crash that he should check into a clinic and dry out.)

'By Monday morning,' Louis said, 'I was fighting.' Fighting drunk, was what he meant.

Then the story became less clear. He had marched out of his office, saying they would never see him again. Back in his London flat, mortified by his behaviour at work, he had (I think, I deduce) combined alcohol and pills to a dangerous degree. A colleague, fearing the worst, went over, broke down the door and summoned an ambulance. Louis had his stomach pumped out, then he was moved to a 'secure unit' at the top of a hospital in west London.

As he talked, Louis' voice sounded slurred, as if he were drugged or half-asleep, maybe both. I listened to his sketch of this latest disaster and I found myself feeling two things: first, that I thought it insensitive of him (perhaps deliberately so) to tell me that the drinking binge had begun with a post-coital glass of champagne – I was still not easy with the thought of him in bed with someone else; second, I felt that I didn't believe a word he said.

This was not the full story. He blamed his illness – his 'black dog' – for his suicide attempt without, as usual, taking responsibility for the drinking that had triggered off the whole sad episode. He wouldn't tell me the name of the girl; he said that I didn't know her. I thought that *she* clearly didn't know him very well, but then Louis had

the devil's own charm when he chose to use it. No one –
no one who didn't know him, that is – would be able to
resist him.

I've been to Rye. Once, about twelve years ago, I went
there with the man I later married. It's an old town, some
of it medieval, very picturesque, near the Sussex coast,
just two miles from the sea. At that time, I had a passion
for the Edwardian writer E. F. Benson, who had been
mayor of Rye. The trip was a sort of a pilgrimage. Rye is
a perfect place for a weekend if you're in love.

So I could easily imagine Louis and his lady-friend in
Rye, walking hand-in-hand through its steep, cobbled
streets before wending their way back to one of those bijou
hotels, all chintz and reproduction antiques. There they
were, drawing the ruched curtains against the late
afternoon sun, pulling back the flowered bedspread,
removing their clothes languorously, slowly. Or with the
swift urgency of desire? I didn't want to imagine any more.

And then, in painful contrast, I had a sudden, unwelcome, vivid vision of the flat, that sad flat with its stained
carpet and its sour smell – sourer now – and Louis lying
there – where? Upstairs, on the white bed? Perhaps not
so white now? Downstairs on the sofa? On the floor? –
the door being broken down, and the ambulance rushing
through the narrow streets of Kensington, its siren
wailing fit to wake the dead.

I said, 'Do you want me to come and see you?'

Why did I say this? Why on earth did I say this?

I didn't want to see him. It would not be true to say
that I was indifferent to him. I wasn't. If anything, I was
scared of him, frightened of being drawn back into that

cycle of attraction and destruction. I also felt repelled: a mixture of compulsion and repulsion had always been characteristic of my feelings about him. Ambivalence. Opposites attract. Maternal and filial. Attraction and destruction. Love–hate. I want. I do not want.

'Yes, darling, but do come in the morning because I'm always doped by the afternoon.'

'I'll come tomorrow.'

Come the day, come the hour, I couldn't face it. I didn't go. Late in the afternoon he called to ask when I was coming, *if* I was coming.

'It's all right if you can't make it,' he said, 'it's just sometimes they give me pills and then I'm not much good.'

'I'll come tomorrow, late morning,' I said.

Tomorrow is the anniversary of my father's death. He died three years ago on a Sunday. The anniversary this year falls on a Tuesday. Even if he were alive, I wouldn't be going for Sunday lunch. It wouldn't be Sunday. And anyhow I'm here in this beautiful, big house in Naxos, watching the sun set over the port.

At dusk the tourists come, uninvited, up on to the terrace to take photographs of the sunset. They climb the narrow steps, the camera (sometimes video camera) already glued to their right eye. They don't even see the sunset, not really. How could they? They don't even look at it, but when they get home they can take out their photograph, or their movie, which of course, looks *nothing* like the sunset and look at it instead and make believe, no, believe, that they have seen the most beautiful sunset in the Greek islands.

My father despised photography, except as a record. He said it wasn't art. You can't document a sunset.

'This is private property,' I say. 'Go away.'

'Oh, please, just one photo.' The tourists are barely polite. They assume I will let them come up.

But I am resolute. I don't relent. I don't want them on my terrace. Even though I am only in this house for four weeks, I feel proprietorial about it. I have been happy here. I am happy here.

When it's dark and the terrace – or rather, the sunset – no longer needs guarding, I go back into the house. I take Nanci Griffith off the CD player and, in honour of my father's memory, put on a song called 'The Living Years.' I very much doubt that he, my father, would have liked the music, but he might have appreciated the gesture. It's odd. I see now, looking at the sleeve notes, that it had been released *six* years before my father died, yet it was a big hit around the time of his death, always on the radio. I used to listen to it in the car and cry. Eventually I went out and bought a copy. I know all the words, but that's not unusual. I always know the words of popular songs. They speak to me. This one does especially, because the singer is singing about how he regrets that he and his father weren't able to communicate in life and it's too late now. I know just how he feels. It's not a great song, but it moves me.

I still haven't been to see my father's grave. I can't face it. I'm told it has a tombstone now. I don't even know what the inscription says. I'll have to go one day. I do realize that.

*

The evening before I go to see Louis in the hospital, I telephone his aunt, Joan. She sounds friendly but guarded. Guarded but friendly. When I mention Louis, she suddenly sounds much more guarded. Also her voice starts to shake. 'I can't talk about him, darling,' she says. 'I really can't. It upsets me too much. My health isn't up to it, I'm not strong enough. My children have told me I mustn't.' She had loved him as if he were her son and he had loved her instead of his mother (*She* is my mother really,' he once told me). Now she can't even hear his name without panicking. I start to apologize for upsetting her but she cuts me short. I say 'goodbye' and she says, 'The one person who has been really marvellous throughout this horrible business is Sara.' That hurts. Perhaps it's meant to. I wonder if Joan thinks that I have betrayed Louis. I wonder if she thinks it's my fault. Was I perhaps meant to save him? If I had tried harder, I wonder, could I have done so?

As I enter the hospital to visit Louis, I feel weak. To stiffen my resolve, I mutter to myself, 'Don't think about yourself. Don't be scared. You don't have to stay long.'

The secure unit is on the top floor of the hospital, six storeys up. On the reception desk there is a notice requesting visitors to check with staff before going to see any of the patients. In case they're having treatment, I suppose, I think to myself. Do they still use electro-convulsive therapy? I realize that I expect to hear the sound of screaming.

In Edinburgh, when I was about twenty, I saw a production of Peter Weiss's play *Marat/Sade*. Mad people in white gowns and strait-jackets, gibbering and foaming at the mouth. It terrified me, gave me nightmares for weeks. Unbidden, the memory comes back to me. Madness frightens me.

When I tell the young orderly who I have come to see, he says breezily, 'He's in the smoking room. I'll tell him you're here.'

Louis walks towards me and kisses me on both cheeks. Air kisses. I almost don't recognize him and yet, of course, I know him at once. He is painfully thin and his wonderful hair is now almost completely grey, though still very thick. His legs are like sticks and he seems to have become knock-kneed. Certainly he is walking very strangely. I ask if he is in pain. I wonder if perhaps the stomach pump has left him bruised, but I don't quite like to enquire.

'No,' he says, 'it's the medication. It affects my balance.'

He is wearing a shirt and jeans. Somehow I had expected him to be in pyjamas and a dressing gown.

Louis escorts me to his room, where he sits down on the bed and lights a cigarette. I sit opposite in an armchair, the visitor's chair. There is a sign on the door saying that it must be left open at all times. We talk – about this and that. He is doing a literary quiz in one of the Sunday papers and has, despite his drugged state, managed to complete most of the answers. I supply one – to a question I now can't remember: the answer is *Flush* by Virginia Woolf.

I know this because I have just finished reading a biography of Virginia Woolf, who was a manic depressive too (but not an alcoholic), and, in the end, killed herself because she could not face another bout of depression. She wrote in her suicide note, 'I feel certain that I am going mad again: I feel we cant go through another of these terrible times . . .' In the book there is a description of her face, pinched and distorted by suffering. When I read it, it made me think of Louis. But it was shame (I think), rather than depression, that drove Louis to attempt suicide.

It is not at all like old times. I feel horror and a desperate pity which I am trying to conceal. I have felt intimations of this horror in the past and certainly I have felt the pity, but always diluted by love and lust. Now, before me, is the wreck of a human being. The enormity of my, of our, failure hits me. Great love, *the* great love, was beyond us. We couldn't bring it off.

I remember my dream about the drunk who stands at the end of the street where I live. It seems, in retrospect, precognitive. What is there now to distinguish Louis from this man? I also feel relief. I have escaped. Louis has not been so lucky.

Louis doesn't mention the car crash or the court case. His version of what has happened to him is heavily edited. Of course it is. The truth would drive him mad – madder. It would mean that he would have to finish the job. Better luck next time, old boy. Louis can't face how badly he has fucked up. I don't blame him. There but for the grace of God . . .

Suddenly he gets up, walks – shakily – to the door and locks it.

'What are you doing?' I ask, panicking. All at once I am very frightened.

'I'm locking the door so I can kiss you,' he says, as he walks towards me.

'No, please. Please. No. I don't want to be kissed.' To my own ears I sound hysterical. That is how I feel. I must prevent this kiss.

'OK,' he says, turning. No problem. He goes back to the door, unlocks it and returns to his seat. We go on talking, this time about his job, from which he is certain to be fired. After another fifteen minutes I get up to leave. I have not been here for even half an hour but I have arranged a rendezvous nearby precisely so that I will have an excuse to leave.

Louis escorts me to the lift and pecks me on both cheeks. Before the doors have even closed, he has already turned away and is walking back to his room. I think he has already forgotten me. From behind, he looks very old.